MW01043577

ALL THAT GLITTERS

ALL THAT GLITTERS

Martine Desjardins

Translated by
Fred A. Reed and David Homel

Talonbooks
Vancouver

Copyright © 2003 Leméac Éditeur Inc.

Translation copyright © 2005 David Homel and Fred A. Reed

Talonbooks
P.O. Box 2076, Vancouver, British Columbia, Canada V6B 3S3
www.talonbooks.com

Typeset in Scala and printed and bound in Canada by AGMV Marquis.

First Printing: 2005

No part of this book, covered by the copyright hereon, may be reproduced or used in any form or by any means—graphic, electronic or mechanical—without prior permission of the publisher, except for excerpts in a review. Any request for photocopying of any part of this book shall be directed in writing to Access Copyright (The Canadian Copyright Licensing Agency), 1 Yonge Street, Suite 1900, Toronto, Ontario, Canada M5E 1E5; Tel.:(416) 868-1620; Fax:(416) 868-1621.

L'élu du hasard by Martine Desjardins was first published in French by Leméac Éditeur Inc., Montreal.

NATIONAL LIBRARY OF CANADA CATALOGUING IN PUBLICATION

Desjardins, Martine, 1957–
[Élu du hasard. English]
   All that glitters / Martine Desjardins ; translated by Fred A. Reed and David Homel.

Translation of: L'élu du hasard.
ISBN 0-88922-520-6

   I. Reed, Fred A., 1939– II. Homel, David III. Title. IV. Title: Élu du hasard. English.

PS8557.E78284E4813 2005   C843'.54   C2004-906437-1

The author gratefully acknowledges the financial support of the Canada Council for the Arts.

The publisher gratefully acknowledges the financial support of the Canada Council for the Arts; the Government of Canada through the Book Publishing Industry Development Program; and the Province of British Columbia through the British Columbia Arts Council for our publishing activities.

For Serge Larivière
and in memory of Major Georges-Étienne Milette,
Chief-Assistant Surgeon,
Hôpital militaire de Saint-Cloud, 1916–1918

Acknowledgements

I owe a debt of gratitude to all those who, of their own free will or otherwise, were pressed into answering my endless questions about the Crusades, land registers, cloisters, oblong shields, Solomon's Seal, meadowlark nests and tapestries: Mireille Desjardins, Denyse Milette, Laurent Busseau and, most particularly, my head archivist Maurice Desjardins.

Soliman, of all mortals, most adroit in the divination of
rebuses and the solving of charades ...

NERVAL, *Les nuits de Ramazan*

... and the monstrous cube of Antonia's Tower held sway
over Jerusalem.

FLAUBERT, *Hérodias*

I

IACTA ALEA EST. Let there be no mistake: the game has begun. I can feel it in my fingertips as I roll the dice, and in the pit of my stomach as they skitter across the baize. Each winning cast causes my stones to constrict with excitement. Nine times out of ten, I win. For the last week, luck has been coursing like fresh blood through my veins. My dice cup has become a cornucopia that repays me one-hundredfold all that I might have lost before.

Around me, the men mutter that I must have been born under a lucky star, or issued from my mother's womb enveloped in a fetal membrane of good fortune. The poor losers wonder aloud if, perhaps, I have not rubbed the hump of a hunchback or consorted with the hanged. Few are more superstitious than soldiers in wartime. Meanwhile, I prostrate myself at fortune's feet and there reap the bountiful harvest of her generosity. Yet behind this unhoped-for run of luck, I detect a design greater than luck itself, the intentions of which are, for the moment, unfathomable. With each roll of the dice I feel I am moving across the squares of an immense game-board, whose ultimate course and whose obstacles I cannot distinguish, whose rules I cannot yet grasp. I have no idea where it will all lead. All I can say with any certainty is that it began last Sunday.

On that afternoon, a series of coincidences had deposited me at Stonehenge. I was to have been on leave in London with my mates, but on the way to the station my shoelace had come undone, my forage cap had blown off, and I had missed the train—by no more than five seconds. The cogwheels of fate mesh with uncanny precision!

Determined to make the best of a bad lot, I jumped aboard a lorry heading for Salisbury, where I spent an hour looking for a dice cup at an antiquarian's, who had little to offer, save a goblet covered in petit point. I took my meal in the town, quaffing a pint of beer to sluice down a slice of mutton stewed to the consistency of boot leather, then struck out on foot across the open fields toward the campground.

There was a briskness in the air, and the wind stung like pins and needles. The hoarfrost that coated the puddles crackled beneath my heels like barley sugar. I was rapidly drawing near the monuments of Stonehenge. Though my battalion had been in training in the nearby countryside for the last four months, I had never set foot there. I might well have kept going had I not caught a glimpse, from the road, of a white-coiffed head making its way between the megaliths. Beneath it I believed I could distinguish the uniform of an army nurse—a cape the colour of a blue jay's plumage that had won the ladies the nickname of *Bluebirds*. Well, well! What would an army nurse be doing in these parts? Turning toward her, I hastened my step.

Seen from afar, the dolmens of Stonehenge resemble a pile of cubes, but from close up, they tell quite a different story. Some stand a good twenty feet tall and must weigh several tons. The megaliths form an enclosure within which stand two concentric circles of smaller menhirs. Except for the stones, the place appeared deserted. Where could the nurse have gone? As I was wondering if she had not simply vanished into thin air, a rustling of fabric made me raise my head. And so I spied her, perched atop a massive, toppled stele. A thought crossed my mind: when the hens go to roost, the storm cannot be far behind.

"Have you also come to play?"

Her voice, like the rest of her person, affected me as would some turbulence in the atmosphere. Her face had a changing quality about it, like a sky filled with rapidly scudding clouds. If you did not like its appearance, you could simply wait a few moments for an entirely different impression to occur—which I was not inclined to do. I had no complaint about her face, except that it had begun to make my head spin.

"Play what?"

"Dice! They say the stones of Stonehenge form an immense wheel of fortune that can change your luck for the better."

So, the lady was a roller of dice. That, at least, would explain the turbulence.

"Nothing plays upon fortune like fortune itself. It's a vicious circle."

"Even if you're not superstitious, there's nothing to lose by trying."

She waved her right hand, and with a languid shiver I recognized the familiar rattle of impatient dice. Her other hand was gloved, and she held it across her waist, as though she were paralyzed.

"Where I come from, women don't play dice."

"Is that so? And where would that be?"

"High Bluff."

"High Bluff?"

"Manitoba."

"And why didn't you stay there?"

How innocently her eyelashes fluttered ... You would have sworn the question was completely disingenuous. Still, she had dismissed me; of that I had no doubt. There was no reason why I should not reply brusquely, in kind, but I decided to remain civil.

"I answered the call of the mother country."

She all but burst out laughing. Then quickly thinking better of it, she looked at me with a knowing smile.

"Just like me, of course. Yet no one marches off to war without hidden motives."

The harder I worked to avoid her piercing gaze, the more insistently it darted to and fro around me, as if to cut off all possible paths of retreat. I experienced a moment of weakness, a movement of self-betrayal. But rapidly I righted myself.

"Disasters have always attracted me. In High Bluff, I would run a mile in the middle of the night to watch a house on fire. As I see it, there is no greater tinderbox than Flanders."

"True, and we will soon have all the fire we want."

Did she mean to mock or approve of my brash manner? It mattered little to me. As far as I could determine, it would take nothing less than a raging fire to amuse this young lady. The fabric of her coif snapped in the wind as though it might be carried away at any moment. A rebellious lock of pale golden hair had slipped free and brushed against her cheek. I felt a sudden desire to seize it, wrap it around my finger, then take hold of her entire mane. With a single, rapid motion, I clambered up the stele and sat down beside her. The war was now far from my thoughts.

"We might as well begin. The first to roll a double ace wins."

Where her knotted brows converged, three tiny folds formed a fleeting palm frond.

"It isn't the most exciting of games, unless the stakes are high."

From my pocket I produced the meagre funds remaining. There must have been the equivalent of three dollars. The nurse quickly acquiesced and handed me her dice cup. I must confess I was rather startled: it was the same goblet covered in petit point I had seen that very morning at the antiquarian's.

The game lasted an hour, perhaps two. We would no doubt have continued playing had my adversary not exhausted her stake, and been forced to admit defeat. I won fifteen dollars— the equivalent of two weeks' allowance! As I was about to pocket the money, the gloved hand seized my arm.

"Not so fast, soldier boy. You owe me my revenge."

"Tell me where and when, and I'll be only too delighted to oblige."

"Here. Now."

"It's getting late. Soon they'll be sounding the curfew."

"Just one round."

"Double or nothing, then."

"If I lose, I shan't be able to pay. Forget the money. Instead, I'll show you something I've never shown anyone else."

I looked long and hard at the wad of banknotes in my hand. I considered the bait she dangled before me. Then I put the money on the table.

"So be it."

It quickly became clear that by upping the ante, she had changed the nature of the game. It had become a breathless struggle that gained in intensity what it lost in civility. Rolls of the dice followed one another impetuously; every failure of the dice to produce double sixes caused my adversary to writhe in impatience. I was blind to the stones around me; they might as well have been horses on a carousel. Vertigo swept over me, and twice I nearly dropped the dice cup. Just as I was beginning to wonder when this race would end, I rolled a double ace. I could feel my heart's blood overflowing.

The nurse bent over the dice to make sure she'd seen clearly.

"Yours is the luck of the devil."

There was rapture in her voice, as though she were relieved to have lost. Her astonished mouth remained half-open. I don't know what stopped me from kissing her right then and there.

"And my pay-off?"

"There's the money. All you have to do is take it."

"Don't try and back out of your promise."

With a look of resignation she removed her glove, pulling slowly at each finger, and laid her left hand on my knee. At the very point where her thumb and index finger met, she had attached a small pigeon feather of iridescent grey. So that was what she had never shown anyone else? I was beginning to feel a bit cheated.

Before she could withdraw her hand, I took it in mine.

"Surely I can allow myself the privilege of a touch."

Though her fingers did not tremble, they could not remain still. I tightened my grip.

How deceptive are appearances. The feather was not a real one. It was a fine silken embroidery, each stitch of which had been sewn into her skin. It took my breath away.

"You have the most curious foibles."

"They are surgical sutures."

"In that event, the surgeon was a skilful one."

"Don't make me laugh. In my trade, I see scars of all kinds. Let me assure you, the most hideous ones are the work of surgeons. Even at the best of times they stitch up wounds every which way, so just imagine the stigmata they can leave in wartime. If only they would allow nurses to mend human tissue ... But they refuse to trust our delicate fingers. With the mass of wounded awaiting us in Flanders, they will have no choice; they will have to call on us. But in the meantime, I practice on myself."

I was still holding her hand, reluctant to let go.

"When I'm wounded, will you save me?"

She got to her feet with a shrug.

"Oh! You ... You've nothing to fear. The devil always takes care of his own."

II

THE CANADIAN CONTINGENT has been stationed at Salisbury for well onto two months now, in the middle of a plain swept by howling winds. Since we arrived on October 20, it has been raining without respite. I counted fifty-five days of downpour to eight grey days—a typical English winter, despite the assurances of the locals, who claimed the region had not seen such bad weather in living memory. A thousand of the 35 thousand recruits have already been repatriated with meningitis.

Such were the conditions in which we prepared ourselves for the *greatest game of all*, as Kipling put it. Our daily routine consisted of marching back and forth to the music of a military band, shouldering broomsticks for lack of rifles, running through sandbags with our bayonets, firing off two or three shots at a target that only our eagle-eyed Mohawk snipers could hit.

As time passed, discipline began to slacken. The men lined up unkempt at muster, stood at ease as the flag was being raised, saluted their officers in cavalier fashion—when they saluted them at all. The Highlanders took great pleasure in driving around the encampment, kilts tucked up, on top of a double-decker bus plastered with advertisements for *My Lady's Dress* at the Royalty Theatre. When fatigue duty sounded, the gamblers would seek refuge in my tent, drawn by the warmth of the rum and the games of 421. It would have been unseemly of me to complain of their company, particularly since I contrived to divest them of their meagre resources. I must confess, though, that I did not feel the same intensity I'd experienced at Stonehenge in the company of the nurse. Perhaps the sole exception had been the night before, when a powerful gust had wrenched the tent from its moorings and the sodden canvas collapsed about our heads, forcing us to chase after the wind-strewn bank notes like so many chickens.

The British majors who would inspect us from time to time dubbed us "The Stonehenge Circus." In their opinion, we might possibly be made into mediocre soldiers at best, providing that our mascots were shot. By mascots, they meant our officers.

An unskilled worker always blames his tools, but still, the equipment we had been issued was unlikely to aid our cause. My boots with their composition soles, conceived for the Boer Wars fought in the Transvaal, had already begun to disintegrate. The constant rain had shrunk my uniform, and it was now coming unstitched at the seams. My khaki cape was indistinguishable from a mud puddle. No matter. I've had occasion to wear formal dress several times, and have drawn admiring glances for my elegance—none too often, mind you, but it has happened. Never before had I felt quite so dashing. With my conquering brow, my ferocious upper lip and my victorious chin, I felt rather like a one-man militia. At night, I slept fully clothed.

In my opinion, the training period was a damnable waste of time, both for us, and for those awaiting reinforcements. The newspapers were predicting that the war would be over by Christmas. I had begun to fear that I would arrive in Flanders too late for the kirmess and, most of all, for the great game to which I was destined.

III

THE OTHER DAY, when I told my pretty bluebird that I was drawn to disaster, I had not lied. Nor had I told the whole truth. I have always been the kind of person who walks the streets with an eye on the pavement, on the lookout for a stray penny. My gaze is drawn to the bottoms of ditches; I shake the bushes and turn over stones in hopes of finding an object worthy of adding to my collection. Without going so far as to rob graves, or steal from the dead, I find it impossible to pass a cemetery without wondering how many wedding bands and how many gold watches have, for sentimental reasons, accompanied their owners to the depths of their tombs.

I take no particular pleasure in watching a house burn. But once the blaze has been controlled, I delight in strolling through the still-smouldering debris, in which I never fail to find a stickpin or a piece of silver spared by the flames. As a result of scouring the ground beneath my feet, I've learned to detect, as if by instinct, the presence of things buried there, without so much as having to bend over. There are times when I feel I know secrets of which the man in the street is completely unaware.

Some might call me a vulture, but I do nothing more than appropriate what others have been unable to keep. Gold that has become separated from its owner falls by rights to he who first claims it. Such is the immutable law.

As far back as I can remember, I have always been obsessed by the notion that, one day, I will come across a fortune slumbering in a hiding place that no man has ever suspected. As a boy, I wolfed down stories of treasure hunts—*The Gold Bug, King Solomon's Mines, The Count of Monte-Cristo, Treasure Island, The Musgrave Ritual, The Man Who Would Be King.* But nothing captured my imagination quite like the innumerable tales of the hidden gold of the Knights Templar. I dreamed not so much of inheriting their riches as of succeeding where so many others had failed.

Anyone can call himself a treasure hunter. But not every man can style himself the inventor of a treasure. So extraordinary is the calling that he who achieves it would warrant having his name enshrined in the pantheon of the great discoverers. It is an ambition I have never foresworn.

Clearly, High Bluff was hardly the most propitious of places to pursue such an enterprise, and so, up until the present, I had been obliged to settle for modest discoveries indeed. Flanders was a different matter entirely. Since time immemorial, the Low Countries have served as an invasion route. War has displaced entire populations that have left behind, buried beneath the earth, whatever they could not carry with them. It is hardly surprising that so many legends of hidden treasure hovered over those lands. Among them, more than a few, attested to by numerous sources, told of the gold of the Templars. For a dedicated treasure seeker, could there be any greater temptation?

Therein hangs the tale of why I hastened to the recruiting office in Winnipeg as soon as I learned that Germany had invaded Belgium last August 4. I would not have missed the war for an empire.

IV

OUR COMMANDING GENERALS finally concluded that the Canadian division was ready for action. One morning, King George V himself passed us in review, and Lord Kitchener, his Minister of War, took the opportunity to impart to us his recommendations. He instructed us to maintain friendly relations with those whom we were helping in the struggle, and that the honour of the British Army depended on our individual conduct. He warned us as well against the two great temptations that awaited us: wine and women. With women, in particular, we should avoid any intimacy that might adversely affect our health. Listening to him, you would have sworn that the lasses of Belgium and France were more dangerous than the Huns themselves.

His speech failed to impress me. As a member of the military police, whose red armband I now wore, I felt certain that women would be the least of my worries. My duties would consist of ferreting out spies, apprehending deserters and any fellow soldiers who failed to respect discipline; of directing troop movements and the evacuation of civilians. And, in the trenches, I would be called upon to fire upon the cowards who refused to go over the top.

I owed my assignment to the armed forces constabulary to the good offices of Lieutenant Peakes, who had personally recruited me. Broadly built and of above-average height, the lieutenant possessed what one might call an imposing bearing. With his imperial forehead, he stood a full head taller than anyone else. His knowledge of military history was as deep as it was broad, but for all that, his view of the Templars was ill-founded. In his view, they had been little more than armed bankers, and not at all true combatants. Conversely, he held the Roman legions in boundless esteem. He confessed to me that he had nearly been rejected for service because he had filled out his recruitment forms in Latin.

"Do you know why I chose you, Dulac?"

"Because I am such a poor shot that the infantry wanted nothing to do with me."

"You are by no means a poor shot. When Cardinal Mazarin appointed a new general, he applied one single criterion by which he judged the man's value: was he lucky or not? Well, it's an open military secret that you possess a luck that is, let us say, uncommon."

As for the advantages of my new assignment, I needed no convincing. A simple soldier must stand in rank and stay at his position. A military policeman, on the other hand, enjoys a certain freedom of movement and, though he might be stopped five miles distant from his battalion, he runs no risk of interrogation. His duty is to investigate all situations, follow all leads. What better cover for my own research than the hunt for looters and other war profiteers?

Lieutenant Peakes was not a likely competitor. Gold was of no interest to him. His family owned one of the country's largest hardware store chains; he was drawn to iron the way filings are drawn to a magnet.

"Just think, Dulac, of everything a soldier carries on his back: his first-aid kit, his rifle, his bayonet, his knife, his cartridge belt and ammunition, his tent pegs, mess tin and utensils, not to mention his canteen, his lantern, his pick and shovel. Sixty-eight pounds of metal! Magnificent, when you think of it! The only problem is that iron attracts lightning. Have you ever been struck by lightning?

"No, lieutenant."

"It happened to me, twice."

The first time was fifteen years ago, he said. He was in the storage shed of his father's hardware store when a clap of thunder sounded. At that very instant, a flash of blue lightning leaped from a box of nails onto his left hand. An electrical current shot up his arm and seized his heart. His skin turned grey, his muscles began to twitch, and he found himself on the ground, half-paralyzed, barely able to speak. For an hour, he lay looking at the floor tiles that had cracked beneath his feet. Then everything returned to normal. Until lightning struck for a second time. Since that time, he said, his entire organism had been in a constant state of upheaval. He felt a sense of oppression, unable to concentrate; he could no longer recognize himself.

"How did the second strike occur?"

"I met Miss Nell."

"Your fiancée, lieutenant?"

"No, Dulac. One of the regimental nurses. That is the chink in my armour. I would throw myself out the window if she asked me. To my great mortification, she knows it."

"She is that beautiful?"

"Beautiful? I couldn't say. But she knows how to handle a needle. And those fingers of hers, Dulac ... They are the fingers of a sorceress."

V

OUR CONTINGENT SAILED from Bristol five days ago, and still the French coast lay over the horizon. One would have thought the Channel was as broad as the Atlantic! Battered by thirty-foot waves, our troop carriers pitched and tossed without respite on the frothing seas. Further on, the four destroyers assigned to convoy escort duty thrashed about in the storm.

Clinging for dear life to the rail, I made a poor sentinel indeed. U-boats had been detected in the area, and I had been given strict orders to shoot the first reckless soldier who dared light a cigarette on deck. A needless precaution, in any event, for nothing could have been farther from the men's minds. They were all far below decks, as weakened by the constant pitching and tossing as I was.

All except for Lieutenant Peakes, who was in fine fettle. The day before yesterday, he had gone to the infirmary to have a nasty cut treated. An hour later he had returned to duty, as proud as a peacock, sleeve rolled up, displaying his forearm, to whistles of admiration.

"What do you say, Dulac? Better than any tattoo, eh?"

On his discoloured skin, like an insignia, he now bore three snow-covered mountain tops. They had been embroidered with suturing thread. I immediately recognized the extraordinary meticulousness with which each petit point had been sewn, depicting to perfection the whiteness of the snow and the blackness of the rock. In the face of such mastery, I could only stare open-mouthed in admiration.

"The work of a sorceress, lieutenant. But why the mountains?"

"They are peaks, Dulac. That which is loftiest, and most noble, as Miss Nell puts it—and also my name."

The day was dying slowly. The storm had abated, but the ships continued to pitch and toss as violently as ever. I would have given anything to set foot on *terra firma*. Heart in mouth, I doubled over the guardrail, rivulets of warm saliva dribbling from my lips. I pressed my index finger against my uvula, but could provoke nothing more than painful spasms.

Suddenly, from behind me came an outburst of mocking laughter that sounded like the mewing of a seagull.

"So now you are a military policeman? The red armband doesn't really compliment your green complexion."

I swallowed laboriously before turning around. There she was: Miss Nell, alert, with a malicious cast in her eye. Her coif, drenched with spray, framed her face, giving her the appearance of a Madonna. Appearances could hardly have been more deceiving.

"I don't have my sea legs just yet."

"Don't tell me the devil has abandoned you already. What a pity! And what sweet revenge for me."

Her head swayed as she shifted her weight from one hip to the other to keep her balance. I motioned to her to stop.

"I know what you're trying to do. You want to worsen my condition. You are neglecting your most elementary duties, and I shall report you to your superiors."

"Even if I wanted to treat you, there is no remedy for seasickness. On the other hand ... "

She rummaged through her pocket and from it drew a small sewing kit.

"Stitching up your lips would help suppress the symptoms."
I recoiled.

"No, thank you. I have no desire to end up with Lake Superior embroidered on my face."

"Why Lake Superior?"

"Dulac, of course. My name is Dulac."

"I see. Lieutenant Peakes must have showed you his arm."

"I knew about your talents, but I must say that in his case, you've outdone yourself."

The compliment hardly seemed to impress her. She dismissed it with a shrug of the shoulders.

"Just a little diversion to keep my fingers busy."

Seasickness was about to overcome me again; I could feel it welling up in my throat. Just then, the troop carrier hit a particularly powerful swell, for the entire deck seemed to shudder beneath my feet. To avoid being thrown into my arms, Nell grasped the handrail. The sewing kit popped from her hand and fell overboard. Now it was my turn to laugh derisively.

"A bad omen for your surgical schemes."

"I didn't take you for a superstitious person."

"You are right. But I believe in Divine Providence."

She turned on her heel and strode off, furious, then turned back.

"Now that you mention it, Lake Superior would not have been my choice for you."

"Devil's Lake, then?"

"No. Beaver Lake."

VI

IT TOOK ALMOST an entire week for the horde of aboriginals transported from the far corners of the Empire to unload our vessels. On the docks of Saint-Nazaire, the munitions crates alone formed pyramids fifty storeys high. When the soldiers received the order to carry them to the railway station, they believed they were being made sport of.

One of them shouted, "We're here to fight, not do coolie work!"

Some of the men cheered, while others began to beat on the munitions crates. The situation was beginning to deteriorate. Peakes rolled up his sleeves and motioned me to follow him.

Paying no attention to the shoulders he jostled, he strode through the milling crowd, fully erect, stroking his embroidered arm with a dangerously calm air. When the men laid eyes upon him, they turned strangely timid, and even the loudest voices died down. Where had the lieutenant drawn that sudden authority, I wondered. Was it his imposing stature? His iron will? Neither, in the event. No, it came from the mark of gallantry he bore on his forearm, which proclaimed in no uncertain terms that he had faced that which most of his men—who were nonetheless prepared to face bayonets—feared above all else: the needle.

Without a word, Peakes cast his eyes all around, then suddenly froze. Something in the distance had caught his attention, something that I, because of my shorter stature, could not see. He turned and handed me his service revolver, even though I had my own.

"I'm handing over command to you. Make sure everyone gets back to work."

And he strode off briskly. I did not immediately understand why the men had begun to nudge each other with knowing looks. That is, not until I stood on tiptoe and caught sight of a white coif fluttering above the sea of heads.

The lieutenant did not reappear again until we were at the railway station, as the men were filing into the cattle cars that would carry them to Armentières. A crowd had gathered on the platform. There were women wearing double-peaked caps, and chubby-faced children pressing tresses of onions and jugs of cider upon us as parting gifts, cheering as though we had already won the war, though not a single finger had so much as touched a trigger. They could only have been misled by Peakes's triumphant swagger.

VII

NOT A SOUND could be heard in the ranks, only the crunch of boots over the stubble. I marched straight ahead in time to the rhythmic slapping of the bayonet against my thigh, making short work of the obstacles in the terrain which would suddenly loom out of the fog. At dawn we had been given the order to lead three platoons up to the front lines, and now we were but a few miles from the zone where the great armies were locked in combat. The bell that signalled my baptism of fire had begun to toll.

Suddenly I snapped my head to one side. Something had whistled by, grazing my temple.

"Not to worry," said Lieutenant Peakes. "Just a stray bullet. If it had hit you, you wouldn't have heard a thing."

I ran my fingers through my scorched hair. Men stepped aside as I passed. I could hear them speaking softly behind me. Like the lieutenant, I now wore the halo of prestige. From then on, I would be known as the one who had been singed by death's wing. Still, I would have appreciated it had he left me with a scar, no matter how tiny.

As we emerged from a wooded area, Peakes silently mustered the men into a single line. Before us lay the entrance to the entrenchments, like a grave dug deep into the earth. There, only the most alive of the living could enter, the bravest of the brave. I rolled a die between my fingers, breathed on it and urged myself forward.

The scene was one of confusion. The footpath itself was strewn with logs and rusting metal plates; the walls were half-collapsed. Dead-ends and bypasses that circled around to their starting point punctuated its twisting course. The lieutenant lifted his nose and sniffed, like a dog seeking a trail.

"Can you smell it, Dulac?"

"What?"

"The fragrance of iron. Follow your nose."

Before long we reached the support lines where the gunners were busy setting up their trench mortars, then a squad of sappers laying duck board. Beyond the entrance to a communications trench we came upon a five-point junction of radiating trenches. Peakes took me aside.

"I can go no farther. There is so much metal around that it has upset my compass."

"With your permission, lieutenant ... "

I cast a die onto the floor of the trench. It came up three. I pointed out the third branch to Peakes. He allowed me to take the lead.

"Go ahead. It's your throw."

We made our way forward, consulting the die when in doubt. Finally, an hour later, we reached the front lines. We had successfully completed the trial of the labyrinth: an excellent beginning.

The front looked nothing like the great battlefield I had imagined. At most, it was the point of friction between two adversaries of equal strength who, in the course of their unrelenting struggle, had so trampled the earth that it had finally swallowed them up. Over the months, the first fissures had lengthened, and now the embroidery of interconnecting trenches stretched for mile upon mile without interruption. It was said that a man could travel through them from the Swiss border to the North Sea without ever raising his head above ground level.

Between the two fires lay no-man's-land—the "Devil's half-acre" into which men would venture from time to time to grapple in close combat. For the moment, the war zone was calm. The River Lys, which runs nearby, had overflowed its banks and flooded the land, making contact impossible. But shots continued to ring out from both sides. We'd been issued strict orders to keep our heads down day and night—apparently the German snipers could see even in the dark.

I first beheld the panorama through the lens of a periscope. Crouched in the observation dugout, I scanned the horizon for the pointed helmets, the machine guns, the trench mortars. Not a sign of the enemy was to be seen. But I knew he was there, burrowed deep beneath the surface, crawling through the entrails of the earth. And with each of his movements, I could hear the tinkle of the Rhinegold he'd brought with him.

Meanwhile, all Peakes could see was iron.

"Look at those coils of barbed wire, will you, those piles of shell casings, those lattice-work barriers ... It's like a park of iron."

A curious description. A park, indeed! More like a forsaken landscape strewn with broken bayonets. The only pool to be seen was a shell crater surrounded by four chevaux-de-frise brimming with filthy water. I could not decide whether a corpse propped nonchalantly against a heap of bullet-riddled mess kits might properly be called a statue.

"All these heaps of metal—don't they strike you as a tremendous waste of hardware?"

"It is the price of victory, Dulac. The price of victory. Never forget Wellington's words: 'On the battlefield, one needs a ton of iron to kill one man.' Clearly, it would take more than that to kill you."

VIII

THE SUN WAS SETTING. Peakes and I had taken up position in a slit trench that extended up to the main earthworks. An hour passed. Nothing happened.

Impatiently, I tossed back my ration of rum.

"How much longer are we to moulder here?"

"Just wait. Soon the nocturnal illuminations will begin."

And so they did. Suddenly the black veil of the sky was torn by a star-light that spiraled upward until it seemed to touch the cloud ceiling. Then, slowly, it fell back to earth, dangling from a parachute dusted with magnesium that reflected its white glare across no-man's-land. It looked for all the world like a lost traveller seeking his path in the middle of nowhere. Seizing on those few moments of brightness, our machine-gunners opened up on the enemy lines, firing through old blankets to conceal the flame, the bullets touching off sparks as they ricocheted through the barbed wire. Flashes of light appeared intermittently on the horizon, as though day were about to break, then thought better of it. The barrage had begun. Two rockets burst directly above us, their sparks falling in a girandole of glittering green sequins. I asked the lieutenant what the fireworks signified.

"Our men are signalling the artillery that their shells are falling short, and that we're in danger of taking a hit. The eighteen-pounders must be re-aimed. Now's the time to move."

He heaved himself out of the trench, and I prepared to follow him.

"No. You stay here and wait for me."

"Where are you going?"

"I've an errand to run."

Without leaving me time to protest, he moved off, crawling beneath the barbed wire. Opposite us, the enemy had begun to fire its trench mortars. Fascinated, I watched as a monstrous worm emerged from a roiling puff of fiery powder. Its feeble whine grew louder, becoming an ear-splitting whistle. Curious: the worm seemed not to be moving at all. Suddenly, I heard Peakes cry out.

"Run, Dulac! The shell is heading right for you!"

Even before the shell exploded, a blast of burning air struck me full in the face and I felt myself thrown from the trench. The explosion rang out, so loud it absorbed its own noise. My ears roared. My bones cracked. Around me, shrapnel drummed down like hailstones on a tin roof.

Someone attempted to drag me feet-first toward the trench. I resisted.

"Let go! I can get there myself."

"You're not wounded?"

Incredulous, Peakes repeated the question. I touched myself once. Then again.

"I'm still in one piece. Not even a scratch."

"There's nothing left of the trench. You should have been turned into mince-meat."

"Call it beginner's luck."

The barrage had begun to slacken. We found two adjoining foxholes where we could spend the night.

"What about your errand, lieutenant?"

He showed me his canteen.

"A half-pint of water from the Lys. Apparently this water has the ability to dye thread the colour of fire. I promised Miss Nell I would bring her some."

The sun had not yet risen, but the birds had already perched atop the coils of barbed wire, and were beginning to chirp. The smell of breakfast wafted down the communication trench. For today, at least, the festivities were over.

IX

CÆSTRE STANDS AT A CROSSROADS, long the source of its strategic importance. Under the Roman Empire, if one is to believe Peakes, it was a fortress—a *castrum*, hence its name. Later, it was the site of the largest of the Templars' Flemish commanderies. But now that our soldiers were bivouacked there, grand strategy had given way to games of chance: the town was transformed into a seething cauldron of debauchery. Even the meanest hut had become a gambling den. Tip-the-cork, cock fights, fox-terrier racing: there was nothing one could not bet on, and everyone was constantly placing bets, including the children. *Sic transit gloria mundi*, as the lieutenant put it.

I myself became a steady customer at a watering hole where one could play *perudo*, *passe-dix*, *cabriolet* and more varieties of *zanzi* than I'd ever imagined existed. The walls were studded with horseshoes, while bunches of rabbits' feet hung from the ceiling. The customers drank straight from their dice cups. It goes without saying that the place attracted the worst kind of people—gangs of petty thieves with loaded dice who were liable to end up with a bullet in the back on the battlefield if ever they were caught red-handed.

Playing with cheaters was a matter of indifference to me: one way or another, I always ended up the winner. It was not long before I managed to clean up on the entire town, which did not stop new contenders from presenting themselves at my table with all the foolhardiness of those spindly battlers who love to provoke men twice their size. It is only human nature to want to test oneself against the unassailable.

When I stepped into the pothouse that midday, the regulars were milling around the rear table. Among them I noticed Lieutenant Peakes, who was watching the game with an anxious look on his face.

"Where have you been, Dulac? They're down to the last throw."

"What are they playing?"

"Snakes."

"Never heard of it. Do they play with three dice?"

"The object is to roll three of a kind. Any threesome is worth five points. Except three aces, snake-eyes—that wipes out all your winnings."

Four scar-faced ruffians, the sort one would not dare lend an ear to for fear of losing it forever, were seated at the table. With them was a lady friend who, inexplicably, was sitting with her back to the game. Those fidgeting shoulders, the coif that seemed to float above the loose blond hairs around her neck ... Well, well. What have we here? If it wasn't my little bluebird.

Peakes muttered under his breath, "It's she! Miss Nell!"

"She seems to be doing penance."

"She is trying to outwit bad luck by casting the dice over her shoulder, as if they were salt."

"Is it working?"

"She's already lost a good thirty dollars. And now she's playing double or nothing."

"Her chances of winning are ... what? One in two hundred and fifty? Not a great risk."

"For someone like you, who defies all odds, no. But for her, it's madness. A jinx has fallen upon her."

"We'll soon see. It's her turn to cast."

"Go and stand behind her, maybe that will bring her good luck."

Too late. The dice tumbled through the air like a bridal bouquet, then fell to the table where they scattered.

One. One. One. Snake-eyes.

Peakes caught me by the sleeve.

"I cannot stand to see her humiliated like this, in front of everyone."

Humiliated? He hadn't been looking. Cheeks ablaze, the loser watched with a tremulous smile on her lips as the bettors' hands grabbed for the money piled in the middle of the table.

I knew that expression well. It was the smile of the gambler for whom the pleasure of being wiped out has become more intense than that of winning.

Meanwhile, Peakes had drawn his paybook from his pocket.

"Do you know what those men are likely to do to her when they find out she cannot make good? I've put sixty dollars aside. Along with what I have in my pocket, I can easily help her out of her predicament."

It was a magnanimous gesture in defence of a damsel in distress, one that would never have occurred to me. To my credit, I knew that my bluebird had other ways of settling her gambling debts. I could have so informed the lieutenant, but I was not about to destroy his illusions. So I simply shook my head.

"You disapprove, Dulac? You must think I'm hoping to purchase her favours. Don't worry. Nell will never suspect. Keep an eye on her. Meanwhile, I shall settle matters discreetly with these gentlemen."

He strode up to the table and motioned to one of the men to follow him. I waited until they'd gone outside, then sat down beside the nurse.

"Well, well, if it isn't Du*luck*."

"You remember my name?"

"All the gamblers of Cæstre curse it. I'm surprised you're still alive."

She stood up to leave.

"Where are you going in such a hurry?"

"To ask Lieutenant Peakes to loan me a bit of money. I don't even have enough to buy a drink."

"I'm afraid he's gone on an errand."

Her look of surprise betrayed no disappointment, which in turn emboldened me to lead her out into the pothouse yard. She followed with dainty steps, which revealed the bobbins of her heels.

We sat in the shade of an elm-tree and the alewife, a garrulous sort wearing heavy clogs, came over carrying two glasses half-full of a gall-coloured liquid, a bowl of sugar and a pitcher of water.

"Enjoy it while you can, lads and lasses. Tomorrow, the green goddess will be off limits. Blunts the ardour of the troops, so it seems."

Never in my life had I tasted absinthe, but Nell apparently knew it well. I watched her execute a careful succession of rapid, precise, small movements, and did my best to imitate them. But for all my efforts, I could not contrive to balance the spoon on the edge of my glass. Frankly, I have no patience with games of skill. In an outburst of exasperation, I let the sugar cube drop into the alcohol without setting it alight, then doused the whole mixture with water.

The beverage slowly turned cloudy. From time to time, it threw off a toxic glint that certainly augured no good.

"I've never seen such an unappetizing colour."

"Absinthe contains copper sulfate—the celebrated 'sympathetic powder' that has the ability to heal wounds from a distance—or so it was thought."

"And that licorice smell ... It reminds me of the cakes my Irish grandmother used to bake."

"Go on, drink. It won't kill you."

I had no intention of doing as the heron in the fable had done. I raised my glass and bowed slightly.

"Come what may!"

How could I describe my first swallow of absinthe? It was like a strip of gauze impregnated with chloroform that quickly evaporated, leaving a ghostly bitterness on the palate. Hardly extraordinary, but not unpleasant enough to cause me to stop.

"Dice, absinthe ... Hardly the diversions of a nursing sister."

"I strive to maintain a proper balance of flaws to strengthen my character."

"Some might claim you are cultivating vices."

"Vices are the flaws of others."

A rejoinder that would have been inappropriate came to mind, but I managed to restrain myself in time. I had drunk a bit too rapidly, and to avoid letting it show, I drained my glass. Nell, who had already finished hers, observed me with a mischievous look. I'd begun to find her a bit shady—perhaps because my eyes were looking in two directions at once.

"Besides, I also have some quite acceptable pastimes."

"I am not sure that your skin embroidery could be considered a parlour trick."

"They are sutures, not embroidery. I've already told you that."

"So you say. But have the surgeons come around to your point of view?"

Her eyebrows arched, and in the blink of an eye her smile vanished.

"Surgeons, surgeons. Were you at Armentières, Dulac? The sector was supposedly quiet, the men were meant only to be on a reconnaissance mission, yet they returned with wounds larger than your hand. The surgeons had never seen anything like it. They had no idea where to start stitching."

"You believe your method would have produced better results?"

"To close a gaping wound? Hardly. But I believe I have discovered another method for mending human flesh."

On her way through Angers, Nell had stopped off to visit the cathedral. It was Ash Wednesday, and for the occasion the great tapestry of the Angels of the Apocalypse was on display—an immense wall-hanging made of seventy woven panels, three hundred and thirty feet long. Nell had been transfixed by the tableau representing the Lord enthroned before seven gold candelabra; a sword protruded from his mouth, and his left hand bore the mark of seven red stars. What had most astonished her was the way the master weavers had so faithfully reproduced the skin of the characters therein depicted, with its delicate shades, its shadows and highlights. Could this effect not be related to the extraordinary resemblance between human flesh and the texture of this particular tapestry? Were one to apply the same technique to sutures, would it not be possible not only to close wounds, but to reconstitute torn tissue? For endless hours, Nell had attempted to grasp how threads of different colours had been overlayed—for naught, for as she finally understood, the key to the mystery was to be found on the back of the tapestry.

"Did you turn it over, then?"

"I waited until the cathedral was empty. When I was certain no one was watching, I stepped up to the tapestry. Just as I was about to lift one corner, a feeling of dread welled up in me. I felt as if I was committing a sacrilege, and that my fingers were burning. I fled from the cathedral as fast as I could."

I'd begun my second glass. As vacuum thrives on vacuum, absinthe thrives on absinthe. I observed Nell through the mourning band of my swollen eyelids. She was absent-mindedly fingering a cube of sugar. On her left hand, the embroidered feather had given way to a satiny scar that traced a paraph on her skin. I found myself wondering if it would be pleasing to the touch.

"Well, if I were standing before a treasure, I wouldn't hesitate to touch it. Sacrilege or no."

"Oh, you ... You have nothing to lose, since your soul is already damned. And in any event, you will find nothing precious here."

"Put no store in appearances. Behind these walls, beneath these trees, a fortune may be slumbering."

That was where I should have let matters lie. But the absinthe had loosened my tongue, and I could not stop myself from saying aloud what I should have kept to myself.

"Everyone knows that wherever the Templars went, they left buried treasure behind them."

I blurted it all out: in this very place, in Cæstre, the Order of the Temple had once established a bank, where pilgrims departing for the Holy Land could deposit their precious effects. When the knightly monks were accused of heresy in 1307, the King's commissioners had sought to confiscate their treasury. They found the vault and its coffers empty. Yet only

43

the previous day, their servants had seen chests overflowing with piles of gold marks.

"Despite the years of searching, those riches were never found. They have not evaporated. They must still be here, in the vicinity, somewhere deep beneath the earth. I intend to find them."

As she listened, Nell removed one of the pins that held her coif in place and begun embossing dots on her sugar cube. She was transforming it into a die. This girl was nothing if not consistent, and that was not the least of her charms.

"That's all well and good! But just how do you propose to go about it?"

"My method cannot fail. I shall proceed haphazardly, and whatever chance throws across my path I shall consider as the clues I need to discover where the treasure is hidden."

"You call that a method? You are leaving everything to chance."

"What of it?"

I snatched the sugar-cube die from her hands and cast it. Naturally, it came up six. Nell brought her face closer to mine; I could feel her gaze turning in mine like a key in a keyhole.

"I shall find out your secret."

"I do not use loaded dice, as you can see. And in any case, cheating requires the kind of dexterity I do not possess."

"Then you must have a good-luck charm."

Once again I threw the die. Again it came up six.

"Nothing in my hands, nothing in my pockets. I've already told you, I'm not superstitious."

"But you do have your little rituals."

She put on the airs of an innocent girl, which promptly aroused my suspicions.

"Don't deny it, Du*luck*. I've been watching you. You begin by hefting the dice, you toss them in your hand, you stroke them as you roll them between your fingers. Then you shake them, but not in haste. You let them slide down into the deepest part of your palm. The wrist gradually accelerates the to-and-fro movement, until it is shaking them frenetically. Only when you've excited chance to a fever pitch do they shoot forth. For you, gambling is what I would call, in polite terms, a solitary pleasure."

When I heard that, I all but choked, and as I did, snuffed absinthe into my nose.

"How can you possibly mouth such improprieties without blushing?"

"One can allow oneself intimacy with an adversary."

"Since we have become so intimate, allow me to escort you to your quarters."

"You could never travel the distance on foot."

"Is it far?"

"A bit outside Cæstre."

"Let us go."

The road was a long one. Nell kept stopping to gather plants for her tinctures, each of which she identified for my benefit. There was woad, which contains the same colouring substance as indigo; coltsfoot, which produces a tender, green sap; weld, a member of the acacia family, which the locals call "dyer's rocket"; garancine, whose bright red root was long used to dye infantry uniforms, and which stains the sheep who crop it right to the bone. Set a woman loose in a flowering meadow, and she will squander your entire afternoon.

Finally, we reached a near-abandoned hamlet. The nursing sisters' quarters, Nell informed me, were just beyond.

"They've billeted us in a place called Rouge-Croix. A strange coincidence, wouldn't you say?"

Indeed, I mused as I returned to camp. A very strange coincidence.

X

HE WHO WOULD SEEK to formulate a scientific theory of chance would do well to admit, as a first postulate, that coincidences may be predicted, and that they never occur singly.

So it was that the "red cross" whose name this tiny hamlet bore stood not only as the symbol adopted by all humanitarian societies since the adoption of the first Geneva Convention in 1864. All good Catholics know it is emblazoned on the shield of Saint George, patron of soldiers, and on the banner of Saint Ursula, protectress of textile workers. One legend holds that the Merovingian kings, from Clovis to Childeric, were born with a birthmark in the shape of a cross on their left shoulder. The distinctive mark may have been transmitted to their most illustrious descendant, Godefroy de Bouillon, the great hero of the First Crusade. Pilgrims, crusaders and the Hospitallers of Saint John—all adopted the red cross as a distinguishing mark, but none wore it quite so fervently as the Knights Templar. The Templar cross-crosslets were sewn upon their white cloaks, their tunics, their coats of arms, and were embroidered upon their every undergarment.

Just as Cæstre owed its name to an ancient Roman *castrum*, the hamlet of Rouge-Croix may well have inherited its appellation from a distant filiation with the Templars. Its name may well have been the sole remaining indication of the exact spot where their great commandery once stood, like a scarlet *X* drawn upon a treasure map. Was this not why chance had led me here?

Of the fortified outpost that would have once consisted of a chapel and cells, a refectory, a hospital and a forge, only an abandoned mill and a scattering of ruined buildings remained. I could not ascertain whether the walls dated from the Middle Ages—all stones look equally ancient to my eyes— but the masonry itself was in a weakened state. Nothing, however, suggested the existence of a secret niche. If a treasure trove existed, it would be well buried indeed.

Inside an old laundry, a trap door led down into an abandoned cistern. The ankle-deep water was as cold as it was clear. Everywhere, the ravages of time were visible: walls crusted with saltpetre, fissured paving stones. And wherever time's offensive had been repulsed, that of dampness had succeeded.

Exploration and investigation are all well and good, but one must know where to begin. As a child, when I hunted for lost objects, I learned to proceed not in any particular order, nor by process of elimination, but with my eyes literally closed. That was how I had made my greatest discoveries, like the gold thimble in my grandparents' garden, in Winnipeg, the first find that set the seal on my avocation.

Over the years, I'd come to consider treasures like women who have been admired too much. By dint of being sought after, they have turned coquettish to excess. They adore allowing themselves to be desired, taking pleasure in their elusiveness, even succeeding at times in becoming invisible to those who gaze directly upon them. One must deal with them tactfully. Cultivate a certain detachment, feign indifference, simulate interest in other things, for nothing quite stimulates their desire to be revealed like the impression that they are being ignored. Then they step forth in all their splendour, without one being so much as obliged to say, *Open, sesame.*

Do not seek, and ye shall find: such is my rule. Still, the most ancient treasures, those that have long outgrown their vanity, may prove more recalcitrant. Judging from the fierce resistance I was encountering in the vault, I was dealing here with the ancestor of all treasures. It would have been so deeply buried, lost in slumber for so many centuries, that my efforts to capture its attention had no greater effect that a feather brushing an anvil. Behind its vast, enveloping silence, its presence was all but imperceptible. For all that, from time to time I could make out a silvery melody that attempted to mingle with the lapping of the water about my ankles. It was an old trick, and it could not fool me.

The water, inert and silent, heightened my suspicions. Its faint reflection seemed more and more like a screen whose purpose was to deflect prying eyes. I shone my light downward. As its beam pierced the looking glass, signs began to appear on the illuminated floor. Circles, spoked wheels, squares incised with crosses, all connected to each other by lines.

The stone floor of the cistern was not at all fissured, as I had first thought. It had been chiseled by a demanding hand that had intentionally executed this curious diagram. At first glance, one would have sworn it represented meshing gears, or clockwork. But I could also see the tracery of an astronomical calendar, the stars of a constellation, the planets of an astrological scheme, the symbols of an alchemist's formula, the cabalistic signs of a talisman. Or even the given of a geometry problem.

These hypotheses not only failed to capture my imagination, they seemed to overlook one capital consideration. If men had once taken such pains to reproduce this design on stone rather than on parchment, it was because they intended for it never to be lost nor destroyed.

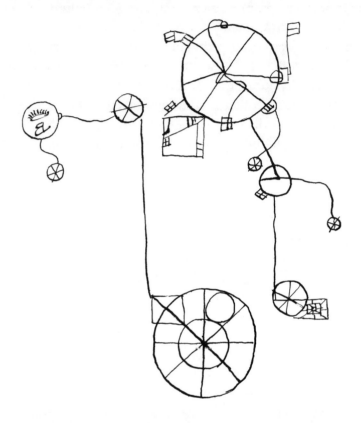

Knights Templar! What did you seek to conceal behind these lines and traces, if not the exact location of your treasure? You took such care to cover your tracks with obscure symbols, so your map could be understood only by the initiates.

Now that it had fallen into my hands, it was mine to decipher.

XI

Peakes ripped at the collar of his tunic. His brass buttons had turned the colour of verdigris. Foam bubbled from between his teeth, and blood poured from his nose. He was coughing up his lungs; had he been able, he would have coughed up his heart as well. A medical auxiliary paused beside him, and shouted into his ear, "Breathe deeply, everything will be all right!" Then he hurried away before he could be contradicted.

Outside the aid post where I had dragged the lieutenant immediately after the battle, hundreds of men were writhing in the mud like rabid dogs. The worst off had their lungs filled with fluid; they were drowning on dry land, flopping like a carp in a fisherman's creel.

Chlorine. That's what the gas cylinders the Germans had launched against us that morning contained. It was four o'clock, and the iron barrage of artillery was pounding down upon us. The men were making ready to repulse the assault that was sure to follow. As we waited, the lieutenant was giving me instructions on how to extract a bayonet.

"To deliver the fatal blow, Dulac, you aim for the centre of the diaphragm, which offers as much resistance as a pat of butter. The difficulty comes when the flesh, once breached, reacts in a manner not unlike a clam. It closes its jaws upon the blade and refuses to release it. All you can do then is fire, which would ruin your rifle. But if you twist the blade in the wound at the moment of intromission, in such a way as to perform a ninety-degree rotation, you can withdraw your bayonet effortlessly, without damaging it."

Before returning to my position, I remarked that the sky had a jaundiced look. He raised his head and pointed toward no-man's-land. A bank of fog had billowed up, thick enough to cut with a knife, livid green in colour. Driven by the wind, it swirled toward us, ominous, ghostly.

"Gas attack! Wet your handkerchief! Breathe through it!"

The roiling cloud had reached the barbed wire. It was no more than ten feet from us. It crossed the parapet. Heavier than air, it billowed into the trenches.

I turned toward Peakes, but he had vanished. I was alone, lost in an absinthe-coloured cloud that stank of the infirmary and bubbled on my tongue with the taste of pears and hot iron. I plunged my hand into my pocket, in search my handkerchief, but my fingers could find only a pair of dice.

I was too disoriented to run. Whichever way I turned, the gas loomed up like a wall in front of me. My eyes began to sting. My constricting chest wheezed like a smithy's bellows.

I heard the sound of a whistle, and in the distance, a voice cried out, "Here they come!"

The dice in my hand began to rattle nervously, as though they were showing me an escape route. I scrambled over the top of the parapet and found myself above the poisonous cloud, along with the others who had not succumbed to the chlorine.

Even through my tears I could see them with their grotesque masks, their pointed helmets and their iron-grey uniforms. Confidently, they advanced toward what they believed was a trench inhabited only by the dead. They must have outnumbered us tenfold.

I drew my revolver and began to fire point-blank.

XII

"I DON'T KNOW YOUR SECRET RECIPE, but you could patent it as a weapon any time."

I was lying on the grass in front of the nursing sisters' quarters, where the men were admitted between four and five o'clock. Nell's tea was virtually undrinkable: a reddish concoction astringent enough to dissolve the enamel from one's teeth, and clouded by unidentifiable sediments. Compared to it, what they served us in the trenches was nectar.

Lieutenant Peakes, who had spent five days at the main dressing station strapped to a chair so he did not suffocate in his sleep, coughed to clear his throat.

"Pay him no heed, Miss Nell. This is the finest mastic I have ever tasted."

"An infusion of poppy is an excellent remedy for respiratory ills. It could certainly do no harm to two such hardy soldiers."

"Dulac is the hardy one, not I. Not only did the gas have no effect on him, he took a bayonet in the side. Look at all the damage he suffered: a mere tear in his tunic!"

Nell, who had paid scant attention to me since my arrival, turned with interest and felt the cloth.

"Take it off. I cannot allow you to leave in that condition."

From her pocket she pulled a leather pouch containing a thimble, scissors, several needles, a pin cushion and spools of threads of various colours, none of which came close to khaki.

I glanced at Peakes, who was staring at the bottom of his teacup. When he had presented Nell with a new surgical kit, he could hardly have expected he would be sharing its benefits with another man.

As I was unbuttoning my tunic, she moistened a piece of thread between her lips, threaded a needle and rolled it between her fingertips for a brief moment, like a penitent telling her beads. Then she began to mend, and as she did, her arm crisscrossed her chest as in a gesture of repentance: *mea culpa, mea culpa, mea maxima culpa.* I was about to ask her why she was using blue thread when she stopped short, needle poised in mid-air.

"By the way, lieutenant, how many men did our hero kill?"

Peakes lifted his head. His eyes were as cloudy as the infusion of poppy.

"Ungainly as he is, it could not have been that many. Besides, miss, the Germans aren't men. They are machines fresh from the Krupp Works—iron automatons with shiny gears that lurk in thickets of barbed-wire, live on iron filings and spit bullets."

"I may not be a sharpshooter, but to the best of my knowledge I killed six at point-blank range, and I can assure you they were flesh and blood, just like you and me. Except that with their porthole gas masks, I could not see the whites of their eyes. Did you know that only human eyes have whites?"

Nell slipped a pocket mirror under my shirt to inspect the underside of her handiwork, I suppose. Her work would remain hidden until it was complete. It seemed to me she was taking inordinate pains with such a small mending job.

"The two of you, at least, have seen the enemy face to face, while many men have died without ever having seen him.

That gas attack was an act of barbarism without precedent in human history."

Peakes raised a correcting finger.

"Not entirely without precedent, miss. Chemical weapons were used as far back as antiquity."

The chlorine may have shortened his breath, but not enough to prevent him from launching into a ringing exposition. The warlike tribes of the Indus burned aniline to intoxicate those whom they were besieging. The Spartans preferred sulphur to asphyxiate their enemies. During the first Holy War, General Pausanias poisoned the walls of Cirrha with veratrine, a powerful emetic extracted from the rhizome of white hellebore. Nor should we forget Hannibal, who had all the wine of Carthage laced with solanine to paralyze the troops of Scipius Africanus.

Nell was growing impatient.

"Let me point out that those individuals had not sworn never to use chemical weapons. Germany is a signatory to the Hague Convention, and now she has violated it."

"Does that surprise you? The Huns have always been a perfidious lot."

Perfidy, perfidy! Such big words ...

"Our adversary has cheated a bit, that much is true. But what is so serious about that? The only difference is that the game is more dangerous. With a bit of luck—"

The lieutenant interrupted me.

"Luck cannot avail us, Dulac. Victory has always belonged to the army that possesses a secret weapon. Ours has nothing of the sort. Without a better offensive strategy, we are lost. If it were up to me, the lowest blows, the worst of traps and ambushes should from now on be allowed."

Her body bent, better to conceal the scarlet thread that she was slipping into the eye of her needle, Nell said to the lieutenant, "What would become of pitched battles and hand-to-hand combat?"

"We should bid them adieu. What is underhanded in normal times becomes meritorious in situations of conflict. The important thing is to win—whatever the price. And, in any event, the victor is never called to accounts."

"Beware, lieutenant. Come peace, your conscience may not rest so easily."

His eyes focused on his drink, Peakes mulled over Nell's words, as though attempting to dissolve their bitterness. When he spoke again, it was in a barely audible voice.

"This war may last forever ... "

Around us, the nursing sisters were returning to their tents, and their guests were dispersing. Teatime had ended, all too soon.

I extended my hand to help the lieutenant to his feet.

"For the time being, the war is far from over. Tonight we move out for Ypres."

Nell hurriedly finished her stitching, bit through the thread and handed my tunic back to me with a smile too broad not to have had a double meaning. I looked closely at her handiwork. Along the full length of the tear, the little vixen had embroidered a ribambelle of tiny, fanciful motifs: an eyeball, a boat's hull, a detective with a magnifying glass, a badminton racket hitting a shuttlecock and a sunset.

"Why the sunset scene? And what does the eye signify, while we're at it?"

Peakes looked at me with disappointment.

"If thine eye offend thee, pluck it out. You've been granted an enormous privilege, Dulac. Miss Nell has embroidered you a rebus to commemorate your victory."

"I am quite hopeless at rebuses. What does it mean?"

He seemed to be gasping for breath, but actually, he was stifling his indignation.

"Eye, keel, seek, smash, e'ens. *I kill six machines.*"

I turned toward Nell.

"I shall surely be assigned to kitchen detail for non-regulation dress. How can I thank you enough?"

She fluttered her ample eyelashes and leaned forward to button up my tunic. She was so close that her coif brushed my chin. Out of the corner of my eye, I could see Peakes gnashing his teeth.

"With your good fortune, Du*luck*, you may come upon some long-lost tapestry in the course of your patrols. I am certain they're still there, stored in the far reaches of some barn, rolled up behind an ancient piece of furniture, encrusted with centuries of grime. Some of them may have been cut into sections to be used as curtains, or horse-blankets, or tarpaulins for ammunition dumps. If you can find one for me, I shall consider my efforts more than repaid."

Peakes, not to be outdone, stepped between Nell and me.

"You can count on both of us, miss. We shall keep our eyes peeled."

We moved off, and the lieutenant leaned over and hissed in my ear:

"Low blows are permitted only against the enemy, Dulac. But treachery from one's own side cannot be forgiven."

I stroked the rebus distractedly with my fingertips. With her sorceress's dexterity, Nell would soon have me wrapped around her little finger.

XIII

Ypres had once been the most prosperous of Flemish cities. It wove woolen cloth for all the duchies of Europe, from London to Novgorod. But its finest wools, those of rarest hue, were set aside for the city's master weavers, who transformed them into sumptuous tapestries.

For three days the city had come under intense bombardment; nothing of its past splendour was left. The cathedral, which centuries of wind and rain had not contrived to erode, had collapsed within an hour. Only its two steeples remained upright, wobbling atop their foundations with each explosion. The clock tower of the ancient wool market had taken a direct hit, and its statues fell like icicles from their turrets into the raging fires that swept the town's Great Square.

"What pandemonium, eh, Dulac? You'd think it was the end of the world."

The last civilians had been evacuated. Peakes and I patrolled the deserted residential districts on the lookout for looters.

I had never seen a more breathtaking spectacle than this scene of destruction. Or, perhaps I should say, reconfiguration. For in their collapse, the stones had reordered themselves into a new, phantasmagorical architecture of disorder, which would have been the envy of the most venerable ruins of antiquity. Where just yesterday had stood proud façades, today lay tumuli, mysterious barricades, rocky, soot-coated grottos, warped iron mausolea, galleries of burnt-out rafters where the flames still flickered. The soil itself was a stunning mosaic of mortar, ash and broken glass which needed only to be stirred to reveal a rich booty of paper cutters, gas nozzles, scissor cases and nail files.

As tempting as those things might have been, they could not sway the lieutenant's attention from his new fixation.

"What about tapestries? Do you think we'll find any?"

Since our arrival, he could think of nothing else. Nor would he allow me to stray out of sight, knowing I was luckier than he. Meanwhile, I made my way through Ypres like a token across the squares of a Snakes and Ladders board, each cast of the die guiding my steps according to the rules I had arbitrarily set down, which were as good as any other. If I cast a single, we turned north; if two, east; if three, south; if four, west. So it was that we made our way from crossroad to crossroad. Five meant that we must pass through a door or climb a wall. And when the six showed, it was the signal to start digging.

We finally reached Tempelstraat. Temple Street. A cutthroat alley if ever I'd seen one: winding, dark and narrow. The further we advanced, the more I felt a deep, subterranean humming. A powerful force lay nearby, deep in the earth.

A cast of the die led us through a heavy, iron-studded gate and into the middle of a rose garden. There, water was leaking from the cracks in a fountain, which had taken a direct shell burst. The floor of the disemboweled pool was nearly dry, and had taken on that uncertain shade of black that always indicates the presence of a cavity below. No longer did I need fortune's guidance.

The lieutenant helped me move the blocks of stone that obstructed the narrow opening. The first steps of a spiral stair-case appeared. We slipped down into the darkness, aided by a single ray of daylight. The descent was steep but short: after some ten steps, our feet touched the floor.

Peakes lit his lamp, and the flame flickered blue in the rarefied air. We found ourselves in a low-ceilinged chamber whose cracked vaulting, supported by four massive pillars, seemed on the point of collapse. In the centre of the stone-inlaid floor lay a massive tombstone representing a knight in full armour. Peakes whistled in appreciation, and the stones sent back the echo.

"Look at that coat of mail, will you? And that helmet! And those stirrups! Iron, nothing but iron, from head to toe. Say what you will, fighting men in those days were better protected than they are today."

Unlike the lieutenant, I was less interested by the dead man's armour than by his coat of arms. And particularly by the escutcheon plate that served as a foot-rest—a large, downward-pointing oblong plaque, in the middle of which lay an eight-spoked wheel decorated with minuscule pennants. It was almost identical to the larger wheel etched into the stone that I had discovered at Rouge-Croix. So remarkable was the coincidence that my brain seemed to strike sparks.

Peakes shone his lamp on the crude inscription engraved upon the plaque.

ME LIGAT AT LAPIDEM
GODEFRIUM MORS
DOMINUM AUDOMARI FANI
QUI LEGIS ADDE FIDEM
CRAS TIBI FIAT IDEM
SED HODIE IN HOC SEPULCHRO
ACCIPIES LUCEM
ANNO VERBI INCARNATI
M.C. TRICESIMO OCTAVO

Thanks to the smattering of Latin I possessed, I was able to grasp the general thrust of the inscription: the customary warnings against death and sepulchres. But what truly pricked my curiosity was the word *Godefrium* and the year of the inscription: 1138.

"Can you translate it, lieutenant?"

"I can try, but I offer no guarantees. I am conversant with imperial military prose, not medieval funerary poetry. *Fani* can only be the antonym of *profani*, but as for *Audomari*? My guess is that it is an ancient form of Omer."

I brought both hands to my head. It was as if I had just received a crown.

"That's it, lieutenant! St. Omer. Godefroy de St. Omer."

"Does it mean anything to you?"

I had no choice but to tell him what I knew. Godefroy de St. Omer was one of the two founders of the Order of the Temple. It was he who, along with Hughes de Payns, proposed to King Baudoin of Jerusalem the establishment of a company of soldier-monks who could defend the routes of pilgrimage against Saracen attacks. Grateful, the king gave them shelter in the al-Aqsa Mosque, the site of the ancient Temple of Solomon. Which is why they were called the Knights Templar.

"This Godefroy of yours, did he not die a glorious death in the Holy Land?"

Peakes's dismissive tone could not dampen my enthusiasm. I was well aware of his lack of esteem for the Templars.

"He resided in Jerusalem only nine years. In 1127, he returned to Ypres, where he possessed an estate, and where he built the first Templar commandery in the West. I believe we have exhumed the crypt of that very commandery."

"That may well be true. But we are not likely to find any tapestries in this hole in the ground."

"You never can tell. One must not cast aspersions upon the good fortune that has led us this far. Now, what does the rest of the inscription say?"

Peakes hesitated. He ruminated. He took so long to polish his translation that I began to doubt his competence as a Latin scholar. But when he declaimed the epitaph in his most solemn voice, my heart all but stopped beating.

> Death has laid me 'neath this stone
> Me, Godefroy, Lord of St. Omer
> Trust in me, O passer-by
> Tomorrow, your fate will be thus,
> But today, by this tomb
> You shall receive the light.
> In this year of the Incarnation
> One thousand one hundred and thirty-eight.

The word "hazard" comes from the Arabic for "die," *az-zahr*. For some, the cast of the die is the perfect illustration of the incoherence with which chance can countermand the dictates of human destiny. For me, it has always been proof that fortune acts on the basis of fate predetermined. By communicating to me this way, I had every reason to believe it was attempting to place me on the trail of the hidden treasure of the Templars—which I'd quite consciously avoided mentioning a few moments earlier to Peakes, that inveterate denigrator.

Godefroy had lived nine years in Jerusalem, during which time he and his companions devoted most of their energy not to patrolling the high roads, but to digging beneath the al-Aqsa Mosque. It was there that they unearthed the ancient stables of King Solomon: immense vaults supported by eighty-three monolithic pillars. So vast were these stables that they could accommodate two thousand horses, or one thousand five hundred camels.

What did they find there? For centuries, the question gave rise to the most far-fetched conjectures. It was believed, whether serially or simultaneously, that it was the Ark of the Covenant, the seven-armed candelabrum, the Grail or perhaps even the secret drawings of Master Hiram, the architect of the Temple—the very secrets that were later delivered to the builders of the first great cathedrals.

This much seemed certain: Godefroy and Hughes de Payns returned to the West bearing a chest, the mysterious contents of which assured them the protection of the Pope and Saint Bernard, not to mention the munificence of the king of England and the counts of Flanders, Champagne and Anjou, who endowed them with gold, land and dependencies. Hughes was soon to return to Jerusalem. Godefroy, however, remained at Ypres—to protect his precious chest, I was sure. Let the devil take the gold marks and the sterling! What I hungered for was the contents of that chest.

Several times I circled the funerary stone, reading and re-reading the epitaph. *In hoc sepulchro accipies lucem:* by this tomb you shall receive the light. I did not believe that Godefroy had been buried with the treasure, but I had to eliminate such a possibility. I turned to the lieutenant.

"Help me open the tomb."

Kneeling hard against the floor, we toiled like galley slaves. The plaque held fast, then seemed to inch forward, resisted again, slid ever so slightly, until at last it swung open with a yawning sound. Poor Peakes slumped back against the wall, gasping. I began to regret that he had accompanied me, but I had to concede how immensely helpful he had been.

While he was catching his breath, I bent over the cavity, trying to penetrate the darkness.

"What do you see, Dulac?"

"Nothing!"

"I don't believe you."

Yet it was true. Not the faintest gleam shone from within the tomb. Neither the shimmer of armour, nor the whiteness of a stack of bones. I thrust my hand down to the bottom, feeling each empty nook and cranny. Yet I was certain the vibration I had felt earlier in the day had come from this place. I can still hear the rumble to this day.

"Aside from a torn piece of shroud, the grave is empty."

"A shroud? Show it to me."

"It's not a tapestry, if that's what you're hoping."

"Give it to me all the same."

He shook the cloth, and the dust it stirred up sent him into convulsive wheezing.

"Shroud, my eye! Can't you see, Dulac? It's a cloak!"

"So what? It's black. The cloaks worn by the Templars were white, with a red cross."

"It is not black at all, it's deep red. I wouldn't be surprised if it had once been purple."

Purple, the colour worn by Roman dignitaries, was extracted from murex, a marine mollusk, Peakes explained. Unlike the by-products of iron, which lose their red hue on contact with heat, the white mucus of the murex turns scarlet when the sun shines upon it. During the reign of the Cæsars, the murex was fished almost to extinction, which made a purple cloak worth its weight in gold.

"Miss Nell will be grateful to me for bringing her this rare find."

I felt no small irritation upon hearing him take credit for a discovery I had made. When he attempted to get to his feet and began to cough, I hurried to assist him. As I did, I contrived to execute a false movement, and dropped the lamp directly upon the purple cloak. As quickly as blowing out a candle, and with the same puff of expired breath, the shred of cloth was devoured by the flames, and went up in smoke. Peakes, still seated, gazed at the scattered ashes at his feet.

"*Consummatum est.* You are truly the king of clumsy fools."

"It's of no importance, lieutenant. After all, it's a tapestry we're after."

He followed me, as if against his will. As I reached the top of the staircase, I peered down at the figure of the knight surrounded once again by darkness, motionless as a sphinx. I had the uncomfortable feeling that something of great significance had eluded my grasp.

XIV

Six weeks of combat and drought had reduced the flowering fields of Artois to a wasteland. Machine-gun fire had leveled the orchards of Givenchy; a relentless sun had burnt whatever green grass remained. Fissures streaked the parched soil, and mirages shimmered at the horizon. In front of the parapet, the sand that had leaked from the sandbags formed shifting dunes. When the simoom of incoming shells would send it billowing upward, the sky turned ochre. The dust lent the dead bodies trapped in the barbed wire the friable look of mummies.

Once dawn broke, the corrugated metal roofs of our dugouts were transformed into fiery furnaces. The open air was almost as oppressive. The mounds of twisted metal scattered across no-man's-land throbbed in the heat like gigantic radiators.

Regulations forbade unbuttoning one's tunic, even under the midday sun; the soldiers broke out in heat rash about the neck. We came upon three men who, too clever by half, had cut off their trouser legs. They were given as punishment thirty hours of hard labour for "having wilfully damaged His Majesty's property." Those who had shaved their heads in the manner of the Mohawks, or in checkerboard patterns, were forced to wear head-coverings made of newspaper for protection against sunstroke. All the while, Peakes seemed to be courting sunburn. His face glowed as though branded by a hot iron.

"How can we not worship war, Dulac? See what it has done to our frail bodies! Fashioned them into superb machines, able to endure hunger and lack of sleep, to walk great distances without tiring, to detect the dimmest light and the softest whisper a mile distant. Soon, iron will be pumping through our veins, and here as well," he said, gripping the rise of his trousers.

Drawn by human sweat, swarms of thirsty insects pullulated at the bottom of the trenches. Even more numerous than the earwigs, cockchafers and red ants were the lice: a single uniform might be home to up to three hundred of them. So far, I had been spared the vermin, for I had taken the precaution of dusting my clothing with cresol, a powerful coal-tar extract used for disinfecting the latrines. It stung, but was effective.

For three days, we had been pinned down by enemy artillery fire. Our only contact with the rear was by homing pigeon, which always brought us the same command: hold the line at all costs. Applied to us, it meant waiting—and hoping we did not suffer a direct hit.

The enemy had cut our supply lines. Our store of drinking water was exhausted. Our throats were thick with thirst, but despite the pangs of hunger, not a man dared touch his ration of dehydrated bouillon, salted corned beef and crackers.

Of all the problems that confront great generals, keeping the troops supplied with water is the knottiest. So it has ever been, since the time when the armies of Xerxes would drink a river dry in a single night. So claimed Peakes, who volunteered me to venture out into no-man's-land to recover canteens from corpses. These little excursions included a secondary mission. On his orders, I was to bring back the finest iron objects I could find—from shreds of shrapnel to shell-casings and spent cartridges. He would while away his idle hours hammering them into useful objects. So far, he had fashioned a pocket mirror and a soap case, as well as a miniature rosary that fit perfectly into a brass cartridge casing. Behind his new-found determination to avoid this shameful waste of perfectly good hardware, I could sense the surge of a love-stricken heart that sought nothing more than to prove to Nell how dextrous he too could be.

The day before, on my return from one of these expeditions, laden with a cluster of canteens and a four-edged Lebel bayonet that would have made a splendid paper cutter, I presented him with a charm I'd found hanging from a strand of barbed wire. It was a cross-crosslet, like those worn by the Templars, but black, with a silver border. On the obverse, I could make out the letters *FW*, a three-leaved oak branch flanked by two acorns and the number *1813*. Peakes's eyes widened as he examined it.

"Is it another rebus, lieutenant?"

"No. These are the initials and the emblem of the Emperor Frederick-Wilhelm III. The date is that of his victory at Leipzig. You are too lucky, Dulac. People may begin to envy you."

"If it were gold, I could see why. But a cross of iron?"

"What you hold in your hands is not any iron cross. It is *the* Iron Cross, the most prestigious decoration that can be awarded a German soldier. A collector's item."

I told him to keep it, a small recompense for the purple cloak I had so unfortunately caused to burn. In any event, the cross would be more useful to him than to me.

The men were falling like tenpins with every passing day. We lost two on each watch. Those who had stopped believing in the protective power of prayer turned to superstition, and adopted me as their talisman. They would wait until I had fallen asleep before clipping off a tuft of my hair, or rubbing one of the bumps on my forehead. Had our reinforcements not arrived, they would surely have gathered my fingernail trimmings and turned them into relics. No matter. The enigma of Rouge-Croix had become my sole obsession. I studied and examined it from every possible angle, until my head began to swim.

It was as if Godefroy de St. Omer, no doubt the instigator of the shadowy intrigue of the tomb, had cast down the gauntlet before me, and challenged me to unravel what he had so skilfully woven. *In hoc sepulchro* ... Judging by the eight-spoked wheel displayed on the escutcheon plate of the funerary plaque and paving stone, I could only conclude that the design formed a map—as I had suspected, but dared not hope. The crypt at Ypres may indeed have been one of its landmarks, but what did the eight other circles symbolize? The dependencies of the commandery? The villages of the region? Nearby sources of water? Forests, oddities of the landscape? What could that curiously crowned *B*, which appeared in the upper left-hand corner, possibly signify? Could it be the first letter of "bank," "basilica" or "belfry"?

No hypothesis could be ruled out, and nothing could be left to chance. Yet I was more certain than ever that without its providential intervention, the key to the mystery would never be granted me.

XV

AIRE-SUR-LA-LYS IS A TOWN MADE FOR commerce, commerce of every kind. It is the centre of the black market, the crossroads of usury, the hub of fraud. No trickery was base enough for the town's petty traders, who had already been selling dear when we arrived. When they learned the Canadian troops were paid fivefold more than the British, their prices rose again.

Of all those birds of prey, the most rapacious were the girls of the Lanterne Rouge, the town's notorious house of ill repute. They could work their way through an entire battalion in less than a week, at a rate of 150 men a day. By month's end, they had accumulated enough capital to retire comfortably on their investment income. Their formidable efficiency had brought them such fame that soldiers back from the front at Givenchy did not even wait for their uniforms to be sterilized before queuing up in front of the wire mesh of the main gate in fervent anticipation of ten minutes of bliss.

Were one to judge by the steins of Flemish beer, the heaping plates of waffles and the array of neckties displayed on the boulevards, one might have been convinced that the country was not at war. In the brightly lit cafés, however, the war had become the sole subject of discussion, in increasingly illusory terms, among the civilians. It seemed that wherever money was in the ascendant, reason slid into deepest turpitude. Here, legends were born seemingly of the city air itself, spreading more rapidly than gunpowder, surviving all official refutations. They told, for instance, of a Canadian martyr found crucified on a barn door in Belgium; how German corpses stank three times more intensely than ours; that the rats of no-man's-land were ruled by a monstrous king in a mantle of vermin; that there existed a magical substance, Turpin's powder, which conferred immunity against chlorine gas; that heavenly archers had come to the defense of the British as they retreated from Mons; that one million Russians, still covered in snow, had been magically deposited in a Channel port in the middle of the night.

In such a climate of collective credulity, in which each story took on epic proportions, it was not long before the mutilated and the crippled were transformed into heroes. I heard a man tell a lady who was commiserating at the loss of his arm, "I did not lose it, madame; I gave it away."

Nell's name would occasionally surface out of this flux of rumours. It seemed that, at the gaming tables, she had acquired the less-than-savoury reputation of being so deeply in debt that she could not make good her losses. This so distressed Lieutenant Peakes that he set out at dawn the previous day to find her, leaving me to patrol the streets alone.

All morning long, I walked the streets of the town, doing all I could to make them resonate beneath my boots. But they remained obstinately mute. I knew that the Templars had passed through Aire-sur-la-Lys. But it soon became apparent that they had left behind no treasure in its cellars.

As I was passing in front of an antiquarian's, noon rang out on the great belfry clock, signalling the end of my watch. I tarried there a moment, idly perusing the objects on display in the shop window. I felt morose, disabused. I was wondering if the violence of the fighting had not made me insensible to everything about civilian life, when suddenly an engraving half-concealed among the bric-a-brac caught my eye.

The subject itself was trivial, perhaps of interest to maiden ladies with a penchant for the occult. It depicted a horned devil, of the kind one encounters in treatises on sorcery. But it had three faces instead of one; that's what caught my attention. The picture, though rather naively executed, was accompanied by a caption that was far from insignificant. It consisted of a single word: *Baphomet*. It was written backwards, with the *B* bearing a nine-pointed crown, a *B* quite similar to the one depicted on the paving stones at Rouge-Croix.

A voice that seemed to have perched upon my shoulder startled me.

"I knew it! You are truly in league with the devil."

I turned slowly, taking the time to sharpen my rejoinder. But no sooner did I see Nell than confusion overcame me. God! How adorable she was in her sky-blue linen uniform. And how serious her features had become. Her expression was not exactly solemn, but there was a certain gravity about her, and her determination had deepened. Pressed by her unwavering gaze, I had no choice but to defend myself.

The engraving interested me, I told her, only because it was connected with the Order of the Templars. The monkish knights had in fact been accused by the Inquisition of worshiping a frightful idol known as Baphomet. Certain witnesses had claimed that the idol was a good-luck charm in the form of a skull that had been discovered by a necrophilic knight between the legs of his deceased lover nine months after he had reprehensibly obtained carnal knowledge of her dead body. Others claimed it represented the mummified head of the grand master of the gambling dens of hell, who had been subjugated by King Solomon and pressed into slavery for the construction of the Temple.

The Baphomet in question possessed six faces, I added, but as with a die, no more than three could be seen at a time. Nell replied that there was nothing exceptional about that; it could just as well apply to boxes, books and any hexagonal object. To prove her point, she pointed to the lookout tower atop the belfry. A poor example, I objected, since it was octagonal: four of its faces were visible. She shrugged her shoulders.

"What does it matter what we perceive from here? I'd like to see the view from the top, wouldn't you?"

To tell the truth, I was not at all curious. Nonetheless, I agreed to climb to the summit with her.

The shops clustered at the foot of the belfry were closed for the midday meal. The campanile was deserted. Nell preceded me up the steps, and with her every movement the hem of her skirt rustled charmingly against her ankles. We must have climbed more than two hundred steps, yet I barely noticed that we had ascended well beyond the carillon, higher than the clock mechanism itself, into the pepperbox turret. Finally, slightly breathless, we reached the lookout platform and stepped out onto the gallery.

All at once I realized that 150 feet separated me from *terra firma*, 150 feet of emptiness. The ground seemed to slide away beneath my feet, and I could feel the abyss in the pit of my own stomach. I clung fast to the parapet, but the falling sensation would not cease. The sight of Nell leaning out over the void, arms outstretched and coif fluttering in the breeze, only confirmed the profound, absolute and irrational certainty that I was about to fling myself from the belltower, and be flattened against the surrounding countryside.

I took one step backward, then hugged the wall and slipped to the floor as the stones rasped against my shoulder blades. Nell turned to me.

"What has come over you? You're white as a sheet! Don't tell me you suffer from vertigo as well as seasickness."

I took time to swallow before I answered.

"I had no idea until now. There are no tall buildings in High Bluff, as you can imagine."

"Decidedly, it's not easy to get you to abandon solid ground."

She sat down beside me, and advised me to look upward until I felt confident enough to make my way back down the stairs.

No need to contemplate the entire expanse of the sky to regain my composure. The tiny azure quadrangle in the iris of Nell's eye was enough. And when I lowered my gaze, the heavenly hue of her dress calmed me even more. My peace of mind would have been complete had it not been for two birds perched on top of the parapet, screeching at the top of their voices. I went to disperse them, but Nell held me back.

"They are finches! Did you know that some species can warble more than eight hundred times an hour?"

Of course I knew. On my crawls through the dives and gaming dens of Flanders, I had not only witnessed cock fights and pigeon races, but also more than a few contests between "chirrupers," as the locals called the finches whose eyelids had been sewn shut to make them warble continuously.

"I'll wager you two hundred dollars, Dulac, that the one with the big crest chirps faster than the other."

I whistled.

"You don't do things half-way!"

"The game must be worth the candle, and that is the sum I need to repay my debts."

I took the bet—why shouldn't I?—and we began to count. My finch was hardly the cheery sort. In truth, it seemed to suffer from melancholy. But two minutes later, its adversary swooped off, abandoning the competition.

Nell had lost by default, that was obvious. But she would not see things my way. She stubbornly refused to concede defeat, arguing that we had set no time limit on the contest. At the conclusion of a long discussion, in which neither of us was prepared to give ground, I proposed a trade-off, which was the only way to save us from the impasse. I would agree to pay her what she claimed I owed, on one condition.

"Show me something you have never shown anyone else."

"You are going to make me blush, Dulac."

"You? I doubt you've blushed since you were twelve years old."

She shook hands on the deal with a shameless laugh, and taking care to glance over her shoulder to make sure we were indeed alone, she unbuttoned the collar of her uniform. Then she opened a portion of her bodice to reveal the place where her breasts began.

On the bluish flesh that nestled between the folds of linen, there was a scar—the regrettable result of a recent experiment in embroidery—that formed a kind of emblem:

I wanted to touch it, but Nell put a stop to that with a gentle but firm tap of her hand.

"First you must solve the rebus."

I shook my head.

"It's beyond my ability, and you know it."

"Lieutenant Peakes would have no difficulty."

"Peakes is an officer. He has been trained to decipher coded messages. Come on, Nell, be nice, give me a chance ... "

She had gotten to her feet, and sneered at me with all the insolence at her command.

"You depend far too much on chance, Dulac. What will you do when it abandons you?"

"If I were to ask myself that question, I would lose. Gambling is an act of faith; I win because I have no doubts. Nor do I doubt that you will give me the solution to your rebus."

"Perhaps. But not today."

"Tomorrow, then? Tell me at what time, and I shall meet you here."

Two tiny points of malice took shape in her eyes, and I realized she was closing in on me.

"As a great composer once said, on the subject of exercises for the voice, going down is harder than going up."

A moment later she had vanished down the staircase. I remained alone atop the tower, my heart beating furiously. Suddenly, from deep in the belfry, her voice rang out.

"Eleven!"

She did not come at eleven the following day. Neither in the morning, nor at night.

I must admit that since Ypres, my hearing is no longer as sharp as it once was. Perhaps I misunderstood what she said. Perhaps it was: *"I'll get even!"*

XVI

FROM THE LOFTIEST POINT IN CASSEL, so claim its inhabitants, one can see five kingdoms: France, Belgium, Holland, England and, high above the clouds, the kingdom of God. The division's general staff had set up its headquarters in a mansion in the town, at comfortable remove from the front lines. Lieutenant Peakes had been ordered to present himself there, and while he was being given some sort of new instructions by his superiors, I waited for him in the immense garland-hung ballroom where, the night before, the officers had held their Christmas celebration.

Amid the puddles of coagulated wax, various empty bottles, nutshells and pudding crumbs littered the long banquet table that had been set up in front of a monumental fireplace. In the adjacent foyer, scribes, dispatch riders and other shirkers lolled about, puffing cigars and drinking port wine to the scratchy sound of a phonograph. Judging from their complaints—these days, on British golf courses, one must now carry one's own clubs because the caddies had all enlisted—it was obvious that these fine fellows had attended only the best schools. Compared with them, I was small fry indeed, not to say the lowliest of the menials. When I slipped out through a side door, I attracted no one's attention.

Though I had concluded several days before that the crowned *B* of the paving stone stood for Baphomet, my quest had not advanced one iota. To confirm my hypotheses, I needed to consult a map of Flanders, and I was certain I would find one here. Staying close to the walls to avoid being noticed, I made my way through a trophy room, then another decorated with elaborate woodwork. Finally I reached the library, which was provisionally occupied by the intelligence services. The room was deserted; I slipped in.

Topographical maps were pinned to the wall, battle plans with directional arrows and aerial photographs of the enemy trenches. The reading tables sagged beneath the reports of secret agents, prisoners' confessions and wax cylinders on which the sound of artillery barrages were recorded. So, it was between these walls that our great strategists met to discuss their *offensives à outrance*, their *attaques minimisées*, their *rectification de lignes* and their *conversions*, their flanking movements and human wave tactics. I had reached the centre of the greatest of all games of chance.

The closer one is to the front, the less one understands what is going on. Up until that point, I had been able to form only a fragmentary picture of my own movements based on the small trench diagrams the army provides its troops. But now, standing before a yellowed, faded map bearing the inscription *Flandria Martis Arena*, I was able at last to contemplate the Flanders Theatre in all its breadth and scope.

I began by pinpointing the places where I had been stationed, and with my index finger I traced my path since Saint-Nazaire. In the last year, I had indeed seen a swath of the country! Yet I felt as though I had been tramping through the same muddy trench, never really coming nearer to the object of my search. Between me and the treasure still loomed the enigma of the paving stone, as unyielding as a strongbox whose key lay unseen right beneath my nose.

Driven by curiosity, I located the sites where Templar commanderies once stood, and marked each one with a pin. Four of them lay behind the German lines. They may have contained clues that would solve the riddle, but how was I to reach them? As I continued absent-mindedly to peruse the map, the tracery of its relief grew increasingly clouded, until I could not separate it from the obscure rebus embroidered beneath the confluence of Nell's collarbones. Soon, all I could distinguish was the outline formed by the eight glittering points that seemed to be dancing a quadrille in the sunlight. That outline seemed vaguely familiar.

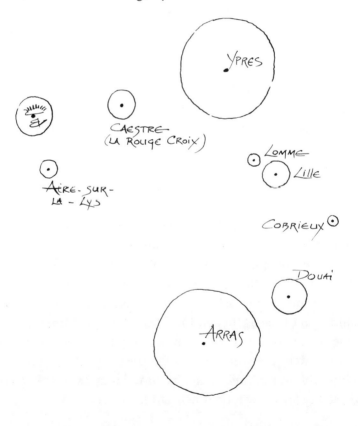

My reverie was interrupted in full flight: the power of the evidence that lay before me nearly caused a wave of vertigo. There could be no mistake. The Templar sites I had identified occupied the same position, with regard to each other, as the wheels on the paving stones at Rouge-Croix!

I rubbed my hands together so intensely that sparks all but flew. Once again, Lady Luck had ruled in my favour, confirming what I had already deduced: the enigma engraved on the stone was indeed a map. But what I had not anticipated, and what should have caught my eye from the very first, was that each of the starry circles represented one of the commanderies established by the Order of the Temple in what had been the old kingdom of Flanders. To say that I was pleased with myself would have been an understatement.

Admittedly, Godefroy—if indeed it was he who had drawn the map—had chosen the most curious of diagrams to illustrate it. It bore no resemblance to cadastral charts, nor to architectural drawings. In like fashion, the lines that joined each point were too narrow to be roads. What could they be?

Everything snapped into focus when my gaze came to rest on an aerial photograph in which the crenelated furrow of the trenches could clearly be seen. I remembered that the Templars were said to have dug an extensive network of secret passageways deep through the earth of Flanders, joining the dependencies of a particular commandery, and the commanderies of a particular region. That would explain the highly unusual aspect of the enigma of the paving stone. It could only have been the map of an underground network, and not of a surface feature. Now that I had realized this, how could I determine whether it really depicted a treasure map?

Nothing is more malicious than memory. Do we not say that it plays tricks on the mind? It can wipe away the knowledge we have so diligently accumulated over time. It can deform words, faces, landscapes. It assures us that we have left the lost object *there*, while in fact we have not. Whoever confides to memory alone the place where his treasure is hidden is almost certain never to find it again. But if he marks the spot with a sign, he is almost certain to have it stolen. And so for centuries, those who have buried their precious possessions have used maps to relocate them. They sketch out the lay of the land on a shred of parchment, indicate the approximate location of the treasure with a red cross, and convey its exact position by means of a riddle that generally mentions a tree, a rock or a well that functions as the first in a series of steps that must be executed in a given direction before starting to dig.

Had Godefroy de St. Omer been an ordinary soldier, he would have relied upon conventional methods to protect the fruits of his excavations. Quite as certainly, his inheritance would have been at the mercy of the first treasure hunter perseverant enough to follow a path all too clearly marked.

But the founder of the Templars was a monk as well, and as such he knew the weaknesses of the human soul. He thoroughly understood our propensity to look with scorn upon all that is beneath us, and to prize rarity over abundance. He would have reasoned, then, that his treasure map would not be identified if it were exposed to plain sight, trodden upon by everyone who passed through the cistern of Rouge-Croix, and if someone had possessed the perspicacity to recognize, among the cracks in the paving stones, the diagram of the subterranean network that connected the commanderies, it would never have occurred to him to seek out the most superfluous part of the entire riddle, thus passing over the only clue that would have led him, as surely as a red cross on a parchment, to the buried treasure.

For that mute diagram contained one element too many, a ninth wheel, unconnected with any of the Templar sites. That spare wheel was the one situated slightly off-centre in relation to the others, to the left, in the middle of which one could distinguish the crowned *B*, for Baphomet.

There where the letter lay on the paving stone—underneath it, in fact—the treasure should be found. To locate it on the map of Flanders, I had simply to draw a line westward from Cæstre. My pencil passed through Cassel and came to a stop at St. Omer, Godefroy's birthplace. I could not suppress a lengthy whistle.

"Found anything interesting?"

I had not heard the door open, nor the lieutenant enter the room. I had just enough time to pluck the pins from the map, and in my haste, I pricked my fingertip. In his new, stiff-starched uniform, Peakes looked for all the world like a pillar. His boots, shined the previous day, shone with such lustre that the designs on the carpet were reflected in them, as in the still waters of a lake. Under his arm he clutched his officer's baton. His free hand held a bottle, which he set down beside me, better to scrutinize the map of Flanders.

"Another one of those archaic documents the French army has passed off on us, printed backwards, with four-hundred-yard errors?"

On closer examination, he realized that what he had taken for topographic signs did not represent altitude levels, but fortifications, towers, aqueducts and columbaria. As for the dotted lines converging on Cassel like the spokes of a wheel, they indicated the Roman roads that connected this ancient fortified *castellum* to its subsidiary camps.

"Claudius the Emperor completed the road network, but Cæsar, who was making preparations for his campaign against Britain, began it. Later, Tiberus, Trajan and Marcus Aurelius led their legions toward the Rhine along these roads. The Romans understood how necessary movement is to successful military operations. For the sake of comparison, look at our front line: it has hardly moved for months now."

I had to concur. Seen from here, even more than from the trenches, the war had reached a deadlock. The sectors that had witnessed the most violent combat only seemed to confirm the stalemate between the two camps—like two gamblers with identical luck. One step forward, one step back, while men fell by the thousands.

Leaning against the edge of a table, he uncorked the bottle and handed it to me.

"Here, have a taste of this."

Thinking he was offering me fine brandy, I made the mistake of tossing back a considerable gulp. But it was Eau de Cassel, a ferruginous mineral water reputedly excellent in fighting anemia, but with an abominable taste.

"Don't start making faces. You'll need all the iron you can get if you want to survive the winter. Did you know our commanders are thinking of using us as targets to draw the Germans out? That way, they hope to exhaust their ammunition. War of attrition, they call it."

"In craps, some players believe that the trick is to keep as much as possible in reserve, while convincing their opponents to place the largest bets possible."

"Unfortunately for us, the Germans are not about to run short of ammunition. Currently, they control almost all of France's iron production."

"Iron is not the only factor, lieutenant. There are the imponderables, things like storms, cold, epidemics. You see, the best of strategies cannot eliminate chance. No matter how inexperienced he may be, no matter how modest his means, a crap player can still win if luck is with him."

"Listening to you, you'd think the war will turn on a roll of the dice."

"The game isn't limited to a pair of dice. It beats within us, and everywhere around us. It creates alliances, decides when clashes will take place, strings events together. You can find it on the battlefield as surely as on this old map of Flanders."

So saying, I placed my finger on the dot that marked the town of St. Omer. And as if it were an augury, a drop of my blood formed a tiny red cross there as it penetrated the paper. Peakes could hardly not have noticed.

"St. Omer is where our convalescent hospital is located. That is where Miss Nell is stationed."

It would be the next stage of the game, in more ways than one.

XVII

CANADA'S FIGHTING MEN have invented a new use for their lacrosse rackets: they are using them to lob grenades into enemy positions with greater accuracy, and at less risk to themselves!

This was the kind of far-fetched news item that appeared in the newspapers delivered to us irregularly by the military postal service. Grenades are tin cans stuffed with metal fragments and explosives, available in a variety of models: the pineapple, the potato masher, the jam pot, the hair-brush and the improved hair-brush. One cannot stand in the way of military science.

If only we'd had lacrosse rackets with which to distract ourselves, our days might have seemed less drawn-out. Of all the forsaken corners of Flanders where we could have spent the winter, Messines must have been the worst. It lay below sea level, at the centre of a polder which had been drained by a system of dikes and canals, but which had reverted to its primitive state under the constant pounding of artillery shells. It was impossible to dig a trench without causing water to spurt out, nor build a parapet without it being sluiced away by the constant rain.

I say constant rain advisedly. Having unceasingly bombarded the sky, we finally caused it to burst. For fourteen days and fourteen nights, a powerful storm punished the front. When the troops attempted to mount an assault, veritable ramparts of water loomed in their path, and the lightning cut off their retreat. The deluge succeeded in bringing about what neither of the camps had been able to achieve: a forced truce.

Deep in the water-logged dugout, the men desperately sought new ways to kill time after I had threatened to disembowel the next one who sang *Mademoiselle from Armentières* (*Hinky Dinky Parlay Voo*), *La Petite Tonkinoise*, or worst of all, *I Don't Want to Get Well, I'm in Love with a Beautiful Nurse*. They organized talent shows, which consisted of ear-wiggling, tongue-curling and balancing biscuits on their noses. They would devise traps to catch the rats that infested no-man's-land by the thousands, then would attempt to predict the weather by reading their entrails. Come evening, they would reminisce about their drinking exploits. They would talk of women and when they had talked too much, they would slink off to a deserted section of the trenches to abuse themselves.

From the observation post where we stood guard, Peakes and I could hear their moans, but for the most part, they simply wept. For the past several days, some of them had refused to get up. They complained of stomach pains, of nausea, of the shakes. Some of them spotted maggots in every spoonful of food.

According to Peakes, our troops had begun to exhibit the same symptoms as the Russians who had occupied Berlin during the Seven Years War. Their symptoms, which were those of acute homesickness, vanished on the day the Empress Elizabeth declared that the next man to complain of illness would be buried alive.

Peakes himself confessed that many things around us reminded him of his home. The lascivious whisper of the coffee pot in the indolent hours of early morning; the rasp of the dugout lock; the scratchiness of freshly laundered woolen socks; the scent of orange and cinnamon that emanated from the men's Christmas parcels. But he kept his mind alert by constant work on the iron breast-plate that he had begun to hammer out.

"An overly fertile imagination is the soldier's worst enemy, Dulac. It causes him to bemoan the past, and fear the future. Do you know what creates a coward? The voice that is continuously whispering, 'What if ... ' Bravery is nothing more than the strength to silence it."

In my opinion, imagination of that kind, that limits itself to visualizing probable events, is a perversion of imagination, whose true nature is to explore the entire range of possibilities. Nothing around me made me think of High Bluff—not even the maple sugar that the Duchess of Connaught, the wife of our Governor-General, sent us at her own expense. All that meant I was free, without restriction, to concentrate my efforts on solving Nell's rebus, a game which was certainly as good as any other.

For all the hours I'd spent, I was making no progress. To tell the truth, the treasure of Godefroy de St. Omer had long since ceased to trouble me. I was utterly convinced that it was indeed the precious reliquary venerated by the Templars under the name of Baphomet. I could not have cared less whether that reliquary in the form of a three-faced head contained the skull of Saint John the Baptist, Asmodeus the Demon or a virgin deflowered in her grave. What obsessed me—and made my imagination race—was the fact that, according to the confessions extracted from the Templars by the Inquisition, the skull of Baphomet was encrusted with precious stones, and the reliquary that held it was made of solid gold, so heavy that only a man of prodigious strength could lift it.

Considering what the earth of Flanders had become, it was difficult to believe that gold could still be hidden beneath it. As far as my binoculars allowed me to see, the front was nothing but a dumping ground where rubbish and castaway objects formed an immense tapestry in which were interwoven the blue of a torn flag, the ochre of a sandbag, the verdigris of a spent shell casing, the ivory of a femur fragment, the white of quick-lime, the coral of shredded flesh, the rust-brown of an opened tin of food, the acid yellow of a puddle of bile, the mottled black of a putrefying mule carcass, the olive green of an old corpse buried the previous spring, and which had begun to emerge from the ground as the earthworks melted away.

All of it had slowly sunken into the great cloaca of oily muck where I waded about up to mid-thigh. And the further I waded, the more it became like molasses, and gripped me like a bloodsucker. It impregnated the fibres of my uniform, penetrated the pores of my skin, made each step weigh twenty extra pounds. I could not but eat it, drink it, breathe it in. I had come to resemble a statue of clay, and I did not exactly smell of Eau de Cologne. The earth had become so toxic that for the slightest cut, the men were rushed off to Bailleul for a shot of anti-tetanus vaccine. To mask the nauseating stench, we were issued a double ration of tobacco. But who could possibly light a cigarette in the constant downpour?

As if we did not have enough to endure, the Germans, cozy and dry on the heights of Messines, had diverted their sewers toward our lines. Amid the drumming rain, I could make out the sound of their shovels digging, their spoons clanking against the sides of their mess bowls, their tongs scraping the ashes of their coal fires. I had come to know their routine by heart. At dusk, they paused to read from the Scriptures, and when night fell, they would recite from memory, in soft voices. Every day, at the same time, they would fire a shot into the air, to salute us. I would answer as soon as I could clear the barrel of my carbine. They had a humorous streak, too: two days after I had shot down the wooden doll that they had set on their parapet, she reappeared, head swathed in bandages.

Peakes, whose ironclad morale was not to be undermined, took a handful of clay and squeezed it in his fist. The mud squeaked through his fingers with a sound that was quite the opposite of a sucking noise.

"Have you ever noticed, Dulac, that the first stages of transformation imitate decomposition? Open a chrysalis and you will never find a creature that is half-larva, half-butterfly, but only a rotting larva. This muck is the corruption of the old empires of Europe, their civilizations, their philosophy, their art. It will not be long before the rain carries away the soil, and only metal will remain. Then a new age will begin for humanity, an age so unlike ours that those who will have survived the war will believe they have left this world for another one. That age will belong to us, Dulac! A new Iron Age!"

I did not believe in this new Iron Age of his. To my mind, when the war ended, the world would be reconstructed exactly as it had been before. And all the useless metal would be buried beneath the earth, where it would vanish like everything else.

"Iron is not like gold, lieutenant. In the mud, it eventually rusts."

Not like the stainless, unalterable reliquary of Baphomet that awaited me beneath the soil of St. Omer. I had to find a way to be sent to the convalescent hospital. But before I did, I would need to solve Nell's rebus.

I pulled out the sodden scrap of paper upon which I had copied the diagram and showed it to Peakes, asking him what he thought. He glanced at it, and as if to answer, unbuttoned his tunic. Beneath the layers of damp cloth shone his iron plastron, polished to a mirror sheen, upon which he had stamped an N at the centre of a radiant sun.

"You're right, Dulac. The game is more than a roll of the dice. And like all games, it is every man for himself. *Vae victis.* Woe to the vanquished. I doubt that your good luck will help you this time."

XVIII

THE COLD WEATHER had come—cold sharp enough to weld
your nostrils shut—and with it, a pitiless wind that shrieked
through our communication trenches. No man could endure
it for more than forty-eight hours; rotations from front to rear
were continuous.

The camp itself was hardly more comfortable. Our huts
were unheated, and frost quickly coated every damp surface—
straw mattresses, blankets, toothbrushes. The grease from our
rations coagulated on contact with our mess plates, and the
metal utensils froze to our lips. The men swarmed like flies
around the open-air stalls where the Knights of Columbus
served hot coffee and chestnuts roasted on improvised grills.
Since the rubber boots ordered by the army had not yet been
delivered, the men were told to coat their toes with whale-oil to
prevent trench foot, as our medical corps called the
gangrenous frostbite lesions caused by prolonged exposure to
icy water.

But the bitter weather was as nothing compared to the
coldness of my relations with Peakes. Our long simmering
discord, which had transformed into open warfare after I'd
shown him Nell's rebus, seemed to grow more venomous with
every passing day. The lieutenant could barely bring himself to
speak to me, and when he looked in my direction, it was
through slit eyes. So palpable was his antipathy that I

preferred to keep as far away from him as possible. It came as a relief when he sent me off to patrol in no-man's-land by myself—even if his concealed intentions were far from praiseworthy.

At first, I thought it was my imagination. No longer. Not after what happened yesterday.

As more and more men attempted to desert, we spent several days tracking down those who tried to take advantage of the continuous troop movements to make their way to the rear. We could recognize the guilty easily enough; they marched slower than the rest. Peakes had become concerned that some of them, realizing that their retreat route had been cut off by the military police cordon, might try to cross the strip of hell that separated us from the enemy lines and declare themselves prisoners of war. There they would sit out the remainder of the conflict in a German camp, far from the constant artillery barrage.

On the lieutenant's orders, I set out to pursue them, in full daylight, in the face of heavy machine-gun fire. The only deserter I could find was a poor sot who had fallen among the barbed wire. A friend back home, who had been looking after his interests, had written to inform him that his wife was seeing other gentlemen. As he re-read the letter, he swore revenge. But when he caught sight of my red armband, he stuck the barrel of his rifle in his mouth and blew his brains out.

I cleaned up the mess as best I could and tried to drag the body back to the trenches. As I was cutting through the barbed wire, I felt movement in the air only a few yards behind me. Over the course of a year, proximity to danger had so sharpened my senses that, even had I not heard the resonance of his breathing underneath his iron breastplate, I would have recognized Peakes by the vibration of his presence—perhaps because that presence had been amplified by a newfound determination, and concentrated on a definitive resolution. As if I had been staring at him full in the face, I saw him stretch out his arm, turn his revolver on me and squint as he drew a bead.

A bullet in the back. So that was what lay in store for me—as though I were a vulgar double-dealer at cards?

There was still time. I could have thrown myself into a shell crater and taken shelter behind a sheet of galvanized metal. Or even challenged Peakes, and given him an opportunity to lower his weapon. But I was far too intrigued by this new game whose rules I was just beginning to intuit. Besides, I had to admit I was curious to discover how far I could go, in the most adverse circumstances, when all seemed to have turned against me, before my good luck deserted me. Would it cause the fatal bullet to deviate from its course? Would it allow me to be wounded, or would it simply abandon me to my sad fate, the better to carry out Peakes's designs?

Finger on the trigger, he held fire. I continued with my task, taking care not to give myself away, hoping the lieutenant would not lose his nerve at the last second.

Suddenly, the shot rang out. I barely heard it over the roaring of the eighteen-pounders. I felt a slight thump on my head, as though I'd been struck by a pebble. The bullet ricocheted off my metal helmet and buried itself somewhere in the mud. I made not the slightest reaction, and let the lieutenant withdraw.

When he sent me into the strip of hell once more, I understood he intended to take up where we had left off.

In the course of scouring the terrain for deserters who never materialized, I became intimately familiar with its most intimate nooks and crannies, so that no-man's-land was becoming my own private territory. I had by no means given up hope of coming across the entrance to the Templars' underground warren at the bottom of some shell crater. Should I have been so fortunate, I would have bid farewell to the army and followed the roll of my dice. In any event, they were the ones giving me orders.

Had the lieutenant wished to continue trying his luck again in the shooting gallery of this immense amusement park, more power to him. I would be an easy mark, since I no longer took the trouble to crawl or keep my head down. Inevitably, though, he would miss his target. Even at point-blank range.

Hundreds of times I had escaped death, and I knew now I was invulnerable. No bullet, no shrapnel could touch me. I needed no breastplate for protection. My skin had been bathed in the waters of the Styx, and drenched by the blood of the dragon of the mists. I was the invincible Armada. Aeneas's immortal aegis. The Canadian Shield. I was fortune's child.

XIX

I HAD BEEN REDUCED to a giant with feet of clay. Titter to your hearts' content, O mocking weavers of destiny! Still, though I lay motionless in a hospital bed, I continued to defy the laws of probability. For I found myself exactly where I had hoped to be: in St. Omer, where I could continue my investigations for as long as my convalescence lasted—and at the army's expense. To have progressed this far, I had not so much as lifted a finger. Or almost.

For six days running, Lieutenant Peakes dispatched me into no-man's-land. On six occasions, his bullets had narrowly missed me. I continued to search for entrances to the underground passageway. How many thrusts of the shovel did I give, only to realize that I had plunged my blade into an ill-buried corpse? How many famished rats was I forced to disperse as they encircled me like jackals? How many shells burst overhead without a shred of shrapnel touching me? Not for an instant did I give way to discouragement. I followed the course laid down by my dice, which continued to point me in a more northerly direction.

On the morning of the seventh day, I departed earlier than usual. I had not rubbed my feet with whale oil, since none remained: Peakes had gulped it all down to keep from rusting. By midday I had reached the environs of St. Eloi, where the night before British sappers had detonated an immense gallery of mines that had been dug directly under enemy positions. Perhaps they had used slightly more explosives than necessary, for the entire landscape had been blown skyward and not yet fallen back to earth. All that remained of no-man's-land was nine craters, the largest of which measured at least 120 feet in diameter.

I wondered if those nine craters were arranged in the same configuration as the wheels carved on the paving stone at Rouge-Croix. Should that have been the case, would I have needed any other sign to convince me that I was on the right track?

I was moving forward steadily toward the edge of the largest of the craters. I had not yet reached its lip when I came to a sudden stop. The depression that yawned at my feet must have been at least fifty feet deep. It looked like the proverbial circle drawn across the surface of the abyss. My heart missed a beat as a violent wave of vertigo swept over me. I stood swaying at the edge of the precipice, too terrified to notice that someone was approaching me from behind, with the speed and stealth of a wolf.

I never even felt the blow. Two arms like battering rams thrust me into the void. With nothing to cling to, I lost my balance and was swept down in an avalanche of mud.

Down and down I fell. Instinctively, at the beginning of my descent, I closed my eyes, and when I dared open them again, I felt as though I was rushing headlong toward the centre of the earth. Stunned by the force of acceleration, it took me some time to realize that the sensation of falling had ended, and that I was no longer moving. I had reached the bottom of the crater, but not the end of my tribulations.

My new surroundings resembled an immense inverted arena, whose depth was doubled by the mirror of black slime that filled it. Far above my head floated an aperture of sky, against which appeared then vanished a furtive silhouette. It belonged to Peakes who, at the very moment he believed he had turned fate to his advantage, had in fact played into its hands. I waved to him jauntily.

"Well done, lieutenant!"

He did not deign to answer.

Around me rose the crater walls, tall and as vertical as cliffs. Once I extracted myself from the hog-wallow into which I had tumbled, I tried to scale them. But the walls offered no purchase, and the mud that oozed from them slipped away beneath my feet. No sooner had I succeeded in drawing myself upward by a few inches than I slid back to the bottom. After some twenty futile efforts, I was forced to face the facts: I could no more pull myself from this trap than could an ant fallen into a honey pot. And Peakes, whose presence I sensed prowling back and forth at the edge of the crater, was not about to throw me a lifeline.

So I began to dig, on all fours, with my hands. Such were my instructions from the dice. I was hardly in a position to argue with their orders.

I hoped to find an opening, a breech, even the tiniest interstice into which I could squeeze myself. My fingers encountered clay, clay and more clay, dense and tightly packed. The leather of my boots, by now thoroughly saturated, had become spongy like peat in springtime, and accompanied my every movement with a greedy squelching noise.

With nightfall, the temperature plummeted, and the icy mud became more difficult to dislodge. I carved out a hole for myself, or better, a kind of burial niche in which I curled up to sleep. Who would possibly disturb me here? I was far below the violent winds of war, crouched in the warm embrace of the earth, there where she nurtures her most precious things. Was I not also one of her treasures? Sleep crept over me. My extremities, which had been tingling with frostbite, could no longer feel the cold.

I slept until dawn, the sleep of the just, then awoke with the unpleasant impression of floating above my crude shelter. When I attempted to rise, my legs refused to obey. They had lost all feeling; they were paralyzed. Hardly prepared for this turn of events, I decided to consult the dice. With the sound of a broken rattle, they warned me to climb, as quickly as I could. I had no choice but to call for help.

It was nearly noon when I was finally thrown a rope ladder. I clambered up from the crater on the strength of my arms and dragged myself to a narrow passage between two smaller shell holes, where I awaited the stretcher-bearers. There is no pity for the wounded at the front. Unable to step over me, the ammunition carriers trampled me; I was no more than another obstacle in their path. I might as well have been a corpse.

At the regimental casualty clearing station, I was deposited behind a coal-burning stove with a good three dozen wounded men. Too weak to cry out, they whined like wet kittens when, by the flickering light of a candle, a doctor splashed their frayed flesh with iodine. Only the mutilated were entitled to an injection of morphine, and then only rarely. Most received no more than a double ration of rum.

When the auxiliary came to me, he had to cut the boots from my bloated feet. The rotten leather peeled away under the blade of his knife. I removed my socks myself; their coarse-knit fabric had fused with my flesh. No need for a doctor to tell me I had trench foot. At the ends of my legs hung two shapeless, discoloured excrescences that looked as though they had been marinating for months in brine.

And who do you think turned up while I was waiting to be evacuated? My good friend the iron-clad lieutenant, who barely managed to stifle his self-satisfied chortle when he saw me.

"So, they're removing you to the main dressing station, eh? Poor devil! May God have mercy on you. It's a butcher shop, they say. They chop off so many limbs there they have to stack them up in carts till they can find a place to bury them."

He tapped my leg and tugged at my toes. His false compassion was so triumphant I almost felt guilty about pulling the rug out from under him.

"You've been misinformed, lieutenant. My case isn't that serious. I'm being transferred to the convalescent ward at St. Omer."

"So much the better, old boy. I am much relieved."

"If I meet Miss Nell there, may I deliver her a message from you? After all, you're not likely to see her for several months."

He chose to ignore the provocation, the better to consider my proposal. Finally, he pulled a matchbox wrapped with infinite care from underneath his breastplate.

"Here, give her this. It's the thimble I promised her."

When I took it in my hand, I realized he was lying. Such weight, such density could only belong to a rare and precious object—a gold ring, for example.

"Are you sure you want to entrust this package to a clumsy chap like me? It might end up at the bottom of some crater."

"Do me this small favour, Dulac, and you'll have whatever you wish in exchange."

"Even the solution to the rebus engraved on your breastplate?"

He gave me a pained expression.

"Those sorts of things aren't given to just anyone. But you shall have it, you shall have it ... "

"And right now."

"What makes you think I know the answer?"

"I have blind faith in your talents."

His chest out, Peakes thrust his face into the darkness, like the figurehead of an antique ship. His tightly clenched jaws made a lugubrious, grinding sound.

"Do you know how long it took me to figure it out?"

"You can take it or leave it."

He jotted down a few words in his notebook, then roughly tore off the page and thrust it into my hand.

"For now, you are on top because you have nothing to lose—while I have everything to gain. But things will change; they must change. And when the stakes become more precious for you than life itself, I will be waiting for you. I will eliminate you, Dulac. And believe me, I will be far less reluctant to act than to speak."

His words left a bitter taste in my mouth. I realized I was vulnerable to the danger that lies in wait for all gamblers: that of being caught out at one's own game, and taking the game seriously. Devoured by curiosity, by the dim light of the glowing stove, my eyes ran nervously over the note that Peakes had handed me against his will.

The devil take me if I understood how he'd reached that conclusion.

XX

So there I lay, wrapped in fine white linen, freshly laundered and fragrant of river water. Every day the sheets were changed, stretched and tucked under the four corners of the mattress so as not to be wrinkled by the tossing and turning of sleep. My pillows were constantly being fluffed and propped up behind me, and adjusted so that the slits of the pillow cases were not visible. I had three extra nightshirts, a hand towel and a washcloth. And all the handkerchiefs I desired. A veritable trousseau.

The convalescent ward was an immense laundry through which, at every hour of the day and night, bundles of white linen passed in procession to be soaped, beaten, rinsed, wrung, hung out to dry, starched, ironed, folded, stacked, sorted and stored. Each morning, five thousand feet of surgical gauze were cut into strips to make compresses and dressings. The inexhaustible skein of bandages was unwound into spirals, figures-of-eight, slings or gauntlets, depending on the part of the body to which they would be applied. A succession of washcloths, towels and enamel basins were mobilized for sponge-bath duty. And high above this great white-tie affair floated Nell's immaculate coif, moving to and fro among the beds.

It goes without saying that before being admitted to these sterile precincts, I first had to be bathed. It was not a moment too soon. I had not washed my face for days, and I had forgotten when I had taken my last shower. When I removed my uniform, the vermin writhed in protest, and when I entered the water, my filth-encrusted skin separated from my body like that of a moulting snake.

As I was emerging from the bathtub, Nell bustled in, her low heels slapping the tamped earthen floor. It was too late to cover myself, and I expected to see her blush. But I could not raise a rose from her cheeks. In this tent, the force of habit gave her the advantage over me, and her absent-minded indifference made it clear that she had seen it all before. I slipped on the fresh gown she handed me and sat on a low stool while she read my file.

"*Trench foot. Frostbite. General exhaustion.*"

"*General Exhaustion?* Shouldn't I snap to attention?"

Without raising her eyes, she continued to write.

"As well as *hearing disorders.* Your credit is still good, Du*luck.* But this time it seems your good fortune has deserted you."

"I beg to differ. I could well be dead, abandoned at the bottom of a shell crater. But here I am, with you, in this place of intimacy."

I grasped her apron strings and untied them. She reknotted them as though nothing had happened.

"Do you call this luck? If you were an officer, you would have been assigned to the finest hotel in Le Touquet. You would have had a private room, a marble bathtub and all the hot water you wanted. You would have completed your convalescence in a wicker armchair on a shady veranda, where duchesses in uniforms by Worth would have seen to your every need."

"I can do without the duchesses, thank you."

"Just as well. Because here, the only visits you'll receive are from patronesses who will treat you as though you were at death's door, and beg you to carry a message to their dear departed."

She kneeled by the bed and drew a long hatpin from her sewing kit. Then she moved toward my feet despite my lively protest.

"I must test whether you have any feeling."

"That won't be necessary. You can take my word for it. Even if you were to embroider my skin, I would not react. My nerves are completely numb."

"Enjoy it. When they awaken, they will be able to hear you screaming all the way to Manitoba."

A week went by and I still had not screamed, though I had to bite my tongue on the second day. At times, I felt as if I were walking on a carpet of needles. But I let nothing show. I repressed my reflexes even when Nell, who had seen through my stratagem, tried to unmask me by pricking me on the sly.

Baphomet would have to wait. Nell, that very charming distraction, was turning me away from the object of my quest. For hours I would observe her taking temperatures, administering medications, giving injections, serving meals, turning the sick and wounded in their beds.

I shared the ward with some twenty others. A few boys barely out of puberty who were so ravaged by typhoid that they looked forty. Two catatonics whose hair remained on end from the terrible shock of a shell burst. Mustard-gas cases who had to wash their eyes several times a day. A sergeant so riddled with shrapnel that he could bear no more than the weight of the fine pekin bed-jacket knitted by his patroness. The man in the bed adjacent to mine had taken a direct hit in the groin; the edges of the hole between his legs had been sewn up in jagged stitches, like the top of a tin of beans. When Nell wheeled her trolley close to his bed, he would cover his face with a kerchief so she could not see his tears as she replaced the silver tube that drained his bladder. Once the operation was over, he would remain motionless for hours, except to moan softly from time to time. In the night, it sounded like the wind blowing through the rafters.

My condition was enviable compared to his. At nine o'clock, after having tucked in the other patients, Nell would apply hot olive oil to my feet, and rub them until they glistened like bronze devotional statues polished by generations of superstitious hands. Then she would wrap them in cotton wool and oilcloth, and cover them with heavy ribbed stockings. Thus she would leave me, feet bandaged, without so much as a parting glance, and sit huddled close to the stove to mend her skirt, which was constantly catching on the corners of the iron bedsteads. At lights-out, when the bugle sounded *The Last Post* in honour of the day's dead, she would raise her head and say, "Listen, the bugle call." But what I heard was "bugger all."

XXI

I WAS FINALLY FORCED to admit that feeling had returned to my feet, and that it was time to learn how to walk again. Two weeks before, I could not venture beyond the large pebble mosaic in the shape of a maple leaf which the convalescing soldiers had painstakingly pieced together at the entrance to the camp. Then, the following Thursday, I was able to trade my crutches for a cane. As physical exercise was strongly recommended, I won permission to explore the environs at my leisure.

Unlike the other cities of Flanders and Artois, which were built atop quarries of rock shot through with underground galleries and caves, St. Omer was situated on an island in the middle of the marshes of the River Aa. Around it lay wetlands, peat bogs and heron nesting grounds, swamps, fenland and waterways. How could they have possibly excavated an underground passageway or a treasure chamber in the midst of this expanse of mud?

With tiny steps, cursing my legs for their continuing weakness, I hobbled down the streets of St. Omer in the hope of encountering, if not the tinkle of gold, at least some atmospheric turbulence. Led by the dice, I visited the cathedral and studied its great astronomical clock. I probed the paving stones of the rue du Griffon and the rue de l'Écusserie, where the local market gardeners offered their cauliflower for sale. I searched high and low through the ruins of the Abbey of St. Bertin. Not a trace of Baphomet to be found.

But during a brief visit to the library, I came upon a fascinating view of Jerusalem under the Templars as drawn by a certain Canon Lambert, of the Chapter of Notre Dame, who had been the master of Godefroy of St. Omer. To the east of the city lay the Moria, sacred to Islam, where the Templars had established their quarters after transforming the al-Aqsa Mosque into a residence and the marvelous Dome of the Rock into a church—the *Templum Domini*, or Temple of the Lord.

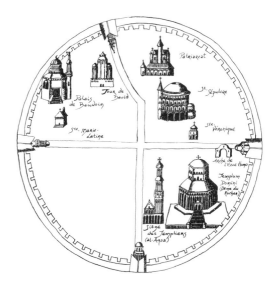

Were these simply nine coincidences, or nine new clues that threw an already complicated web into greater confusion? Clearly, if the diagram were to be believed, the holy places of Jerusalem were, like the Templar sites of Flanders, arranged in the same way as the wheel-shaped figures etched into the stone of Rouge-Croix.

Lights-out had sounded, but everyone had fallen asleep long before. Nell entered the ward and approached my bed without a sound.

"What are you doing, still awake? It's after eleven. You should try to get some sleep."

She leaned over my bed to extinguish the lamp. She was so near, so within reach.

"I would like to, but not alone."

I caught her by her skirt and pulled her toward me. She sat heavily on the edge of the bed with a sigh of resignation.

"The head nurse warned me, when I began here, that there is nothing more brazen than a man who has recovered the use of his limbs."

"I have a prerogative that allows me a certain boldness."

"And what might that be?"

"I hold the solution to your rebus."

"Don't try to convince me that you discovered it by yourself. And even if you had, Lieutenant Peakes got there before you— and he was gracious enough not to claim his recompense."

She yawned and stretched. Then got to her feet. If I could not find some way of keeping her, she would slip through my fingers once more.

"I'll just have to trust my tuck—I mean, *luck*."

That was the wrong strategy. With more than her usual efficiency, she pulled the sheets of my bed so tightly that my arms were pinned down. As she folded the blanket under the mattress, her meticulous hand encountered, unfortunately, just what I was trying to conceal: that damned matchbox I had hidden. There was nothing to do but own up.

"It's for you. From the lieutenant."

She sat down beside me again, shook the gift-box like a dice cup, then, hesitating, untied the ribbon, slid back the lid and inverted the box in the palm of her hand. To my astonishment what fell from it was not a gold ring, but a thimble. A black thimble trimmed with silver, bearing the letters *FW*, a crown and an oak leaf cluster with two acorns.

So that's what Peakes had done with the precious iron cross he had valued so highly. He had cut it, twisted it, soldered it, hammered it, with the sole intent of creating a piece of armour with which his sorceress might protect her delicate fingers. Unaware of the sacrifice that this thimble had cost, she slipped it carelessly onto the tip of her index finger, surprised that it fit her like a glove.

If you asked me, it fit her like a wedding ring.

"Do you know what the lieutenant says?"

"What does he say?"

"That you are the only chink in his armour."

She shook her head.

"Dear Peakes ... "

In the caress of her voice, there was a note of indulgence that suggested that, despite her affection for the lieutenant, her heart was still wavering.

"If he had given you real dice as a gift, we could have had a game."

"Such an idea would never enter his mind."

"Why not?"

"The lieutenant does not like gambling, except when he can allow me to win, while you ... "

She fell silent, just as she was about to concede me an advantage. The silence that settled upon us was charitable to me. The midnight hour—that rings only once—was almost upon us. Nell had begun to vacillate, her vigilance to ebb. I worked my arms free from their linen bindings and took hold of the pale gold strand of hair that hung upon her neck. I went to kiss her, but she turned her head as my lips touched her, and they brushed instead the starched folds of her white coif. The next moment, she had slipped away.

"Enough for today."

"Tomorrow, I shall pursue my course."

"I am free in the afternoon. I had planned to visit the forest of Clairmarais. You may accompany me if you wish."

"What will we do there?"

"Walk. There are centuries-old oaks, and seven ponds that were once used by the monks. The best known is Harchelles, but to have a good view of the ruins of the old abbey, we must penetrate the very heart of the forest, where the pond of Harbaussan lies."

I cried out loudly enough to awaken the entire ward.

"What pond, again?"

"Harbaussan."

Harbaussan ... The pond of Harbaussan. The syllables fluttered from Nell's lips, then dispersed and came together to form the word *Baussant*.

Baussant! That was the name of the black-and-white Templar flag!

XXII

WE WANDERED, LOST, THROUGH the forest of Clairmarais before coming upon the ruins of the abbey. My feet were a tissue of pain, but I did not propose the dice as a way of finding our path. I was happy enough to follow along behind Nell, who was in no hurry. This was her first leave in more than two months, and she was fully enjoying that sense of nervous anticipation stirred by our outing.

I knew we had reached our destination before I spied the ruins. With its tangled undergrowth, its palisade of reeds and its profusion of water-lilies, Harbaussan Pond had the veiled, elusive look of those places that have something to hide.

Of the ancient abbey, nothing remained but the lime kilns, a few scattered walls and the huge kitchen chimney shrouded by a cloak of ivy. Beneath the canopy of cloud, the silence that seemed to rise from the stones created something like the intimacy of a long-locked room.

As we were making a path through the bramble bushes, something rose up from alongside the chimney. I spied the head of a bird, as black as soot, protruding from the foliage, clutching in its beak a long thread that glittered in the light. Nell turned to me.

"A magpie. She's protecting her nest."

"Her nest? I don't believe so."

"Don't disturb her."

Ignoring her protests, I took a step forward. Just as quickly the magpie took flight, its raucous cry rending the air. I had only to bend over and pick up what she had let drop. It was a golden thread.

With the back of my hand, I pushed aside the curtain of ivy, and the chimney wall stood revealed, decorated, as was the custom in certain Flemish monasteries, with a sculpted wheel of fortune, so the monks would never lose sight of the endless vicissitudes of human life. At the centre of the fireplace, a weakness in the masonry had caused one of the stones to become dislodged; something gleamed at the back of the cavity. I was too impatient to be gallant, and was not about to allow Nell the honour of extracting the treasure from its hiding place.

I hardly expected the reliquary of Baphomet to appear in so slight a cavity. But I had certainly hoped to find more than this handful of coins in a long, dust-clogged scrap of cloth from which the magpie had plucked a thread. If it were any consolation, the coins appeared to be silver, but so tarnished it was impossible to determine which side was which.

Nell, meanwhile, was anything but delighted. Hastily, she picked up the piece of cloth I had cast aside. As she felt its embossed surface through the thick layer of filth, she was convinced she could distinguish the weave of a tapestry.

"It might be one of those shrouds embroidered with the effigies of souls that the Christians of the Orient once used to wrap their dead."

"That doesn't explain where the bird found the golden thread."

She asked me to lend it to her for a moment. As she examined it, I admired her porcelain silhouette, thinking of all the ways I might misbehave. And as though she had read my thoughts, she moved closer.

"Certain fabrics, reserved for the dwellings of the nobility, contained not only the finest woolens of Ypres, but also silk, silver and gold from Cyprus."

My hand, which had slipped behind Nell's back, caught the edge of her coif between thumb and index, and gave it a gentle tug, so as to pull it off. But the coif clung obstinately to the pins that held it in place.

"Do you think this old scrap is woven from gold thread?"

"I wouldn't dare hope as much. It would be a miracle for it to have escaped the flames. During the Hundred Years War, looters systematically burned all the tapestries to extract their precious metals."

I quickly let go of her coif.

"Extract gold from a tapestry? That never occurred to me. Let's burn it, now!"

"Under no circumstances."

"I found it. I have every right."

"Since you threw it away, it no longer belongs to you. You have nothing to say about it."

Argue as I might, she would not yield. Made impatient by her stubbornness, I committed the impropriety of giving a stiff pull on her coif, and to my great dismay, it tore with the crackling of a dead leaf. Thus I beheld, between the folds of white linen, a skein of her hair that gleamed like purest gold.

She showed no annoyance, and made not the slightest angry gesture. It was an excellent opportunity to do some mending, she said, and with a perfectly shameless smile she laid her head against my chest. My face buried in her coif, I carried her off into the brambles, whispering all the foolish little nothings I could think of for the sheer pleasure of the intimacy.

I held her close for the longest time, even if the sharp bone of her elbow was jabbing me in the ribs. Outwardly I was calm, with my eyes focused on a point in the distance, which meant I was unable to look at her as much as I would have wished. Her face was so inclined that I could hardly make out the undulations of her lips. And when she attempted to wiggle free, I understood that I had not truly captured her.

I spent the better part of that evening rubbing the silver coins with a bit of soda that Nell had obtained for me. They dated from ancient times. How much would they fetch from a numismatist? On the obverse side was the effigy of a king on his throne, holding a sceptre the tip of which bore a fleur-de-lys. The reverse, without ornament, carried these words:

BALDUINUS ✠ HIERUS ✠ REX

Peakes could surely have translated these words better than I, who could only make out: *Baldwin, Holy King*. But all that could wait. Tonight, only one thing mattered: where had my little bluebird flown?

XXIII

I FOUND HER in a far corner of the laundry, sleeves rolled up, thrusting her arms with mechanical regularity into a washtub foaming with soapsuds. Through the steam that rose into the frigid air, I noticed with regret that her carefully mended coif once again stood guard, like an importunate chaperone, over any stray wisps of hair. There in the darkness, the torpor of the silence made me feel that it was late indeed—particularly since it seemed I had been waiting forever. But it could not even have been midnight.

"Do you never rest?"

"When I rest, I don't know what to do with my hands. In any event, I like staying awake through the night. Some things reveal themselves only at night. Tapestries, for instance ... "

Without bothering to wring out the twisted fabric that she had just finished rinsing, Nell unrolled it, still dripping, before my eyes. Proper drying would have made it easier to appreciate its colours, if not the principal motif: a castle embroidered in gold thread which, even under the dim light of the lamp, shone with incomparable brilliance against the dark background.

I recognized that castle! I had seen it, hardly a few days ago, on the precious parchment in the library of Saint Omer. It represented a view of Jerusalem. For all its clumsy outlines, which would have been due as much to the artist's ungoverned impulse as to the irregularity of the sodden linen backing, its peculiarities had been rendered with the greatest attention to detail. One could clearly distinguish the portcullis, the two latticework windows, the ribbed dome of the tower, at the top of which stood a weather vane in the form of a crescent.

So, this was the castle on both the tapestry and the parchment ... The likeness of the king, and the legend on the coins ... The crowned *B* on the circular paving stone ... Unexpectedly, these elements began to jostle together in my mind with all the urgency of dice being shaken in a cup. Then suddenly, the truth lay revealed before me in all its glorious clarity, as though in a single winning toss.

"Baudoin's castle!"

Nell, who did not know whom I was talking about, asked for explanations.

"Baudoin was the second ruler of the Latin Kingdom of Jerusalem. He is the one depicted on the silver coins we found: *Balduinus Hierusalem Rex*. This palace is the one he had built in the Holy City."

"And just when did he rule, this Baudoin of yours?"

"At the beginning of the twelfth century. He made his place in history by giving the Templars control over the roads, and providing them with a residence on the site of Solomon's Temple."

Hearing that, Nell straightened her torso with a ceremonious air, and with infinite care, she went to spread the strip of fabric on the table. She scrutinized the image, then turned the tapestry over. Her entire attitude changed.

"It's just not my lucky day! This is nothing but an embroidery, like the so-called Bayeux tapestry."

As if struck by disappointment, her body began to show signs of fatigue. She sat down on the table to rest, and crossed her legs. I had chosen a low stool, directly opposite her, so that her crossed leg, as she swung it back and forth, occasionally grazed my shoulder. The opportunity was too good to miss. I snatched her ankle on the fly, and set myself to unlacing her boot.

Mathematicians, who often find pleasure in the most arcane pursuits, estimate that there are forty-three thousand possible ways to lace two rows of six eyelets. But none of them, I could have sworn, would ever have imagined the variant that Nell had conjured up. Her ankle-boots displayed the most inextricable lacing patterns one could possibly imagine: a delicate cross-hatching of puffs, scallops and chain stitches whose ornamental knots challenged me, with an insolent arabesque, to attack.

One-quarter hour for each foot. That was the time it took my lumpish but patient fingers to undo her handiwork. I would have completed the task more quickly had not Nell, from her perch, all the while giving me contradictory instructions, begun to draw back the hem of her skirt to reveal her legs—which were as spindly as stilts, I might add. For my incredulous eyes could not help but be drawn to the captivating reliquary of her stockings.

Reliquary may not be the proper term, but how else to describe the medallions that Nell, lacking gold thread, had embroidered on this canvas of white silk, using her own hair? Within the oval frame of each medallion lay the initial *N*, ornamented by a whimsy of bowknots, and surrounded by a swarm of bees.

"An emblem, so it would seem?"

"A rebus as well."

"Of course. With you, nothing is ever simple. Why must you always create complications?"

"Because I am difficult."

"Don't expect me to fathom your charades at this late hour. I eagerly give up."

Her pupils, which had drawn down in size to the circumference of pin-heads, darted industriously back and forth, binding her eyes to mine with all the tension of a thread stretched to the breaking point. For a moment she seemed to hesitate. Then, some argument favourable to me must have suddenly taken hold of her, for she leaned forward slightly and her lips articulated, without pronouncing it, the key that would unlock her door.

"Bee knots low."

Be not slow!

I did not wonder long whether to take her at her word. With a rapid, steady hand, taking care to leave her coif in place, I sent her apron and her dress flying, then, as quick as that, her shift. But I could go no farther. I was utterly taken aback.

I thought I had seen everything. And I thought I had come to the last act of her extravagances, but I had not considered the grand finale: her corset. Across the laces firmly knotted in their hooks, she had woven the finest of silk thread into military stripes composed of seven ivy leaves of brightest green.

This time, I would not be denied. Rebus or not, I drew my pocket knife and sliced through the knots, one after another.

The lamp oil had almost run dry, and I could see none close at hand, but that was without importance. I felt Nell's evasive beauty slipping between my fingers. I had a brief, charitable thought for Peakes, who could surely never have imagined my stroke of luck. But only when I had descended into Nell's tapestry-lined palace could I truly measure the breadth and depth of my unexpected good fortune.

It was to be short-lived. I allowed myself to be carried away by my fervour, and always in such cases, the results were hardly glorious. Nell shook herself briefly before rapidly getting dressed. It took her three attempts to replace her coif.

"I must be rather disheveled."

She was not the only one. I should have been reflecting on King Baudoin, and on what followed from the evening's discovery. But Nell had taken over my thoughts.

I was beginning to conclude that the hunt for Baphomet was a dead end. That was of no great import now. Doesn't any real search for treasure always hold its share of blind alleys? St. Omer was perhaps no more than a delay, a momentary setback, a wrong turn. To correct the error, I needed only to retrace my steps.

XXIV

THERE IS NO SUCH THING as a single, isolated moment of
weakness, an exception—a single cigarette, a single drink, a
single throw of the dice, a single night. The first indulgence
forms the beginning link in a chain, and no act of the will, no
matter how resolute, can repress the blind instinct to duplicate
it, to multiply and perpetuate it without respite. On the night
I sought out Nell in the laundry, I swore an oath to myself:
"Just once." An oath I could not honour. "Just once" had
become "Just once more," then "Another, then another again."
By now I had lost all count.

Which of us had led the other on? Nell's unhealthy
influence asserted itself like a contagion, as she matched my
darkest urgings in a constant upping of the ante of trans-
gression. We stole time together by dark of night, but also by
light of day, in the depths of ravines, in thickets, against tree
stumps. We needed only a moment, but after each time, my
nerves felt broken. No sooner had Nell and I parted company
than I began to desire her once more, and anticipation of our
next encounter tormented me. Passion, in this respect, is like
war: interminable periods of counting the minutes, punctuated
by bursts of furious hand-to-hand combat.

And now, it appeared there might well never be another
time, only a bitter had-once-been—all the fault of Peakes.

The bane of my existence showed up one morning at daybreak to inform me that he had convinced the head physician to release me without further delay. Of course, I knew well that sooner or later I would have to relinquish my bed to one of the thousands of wounded admitted every day, especially since my newly-restored vigour had come to border on indecency amid so much suffering. But I had not expected to have to decamp so soon.

As I was buckling my haversack, Nell came into the ward. Peakes leaped to his feet and bowed respectfully, then slowly straightened up, tucking his officer's baton under his arm, so as to draw attention to his height, the circumference of his chest and the slimness of his silhouette. Erect, straight as a ramrod, he stood a good head taller than I, and you had to open your eyes wide to take him in with a single glance. His self-control was admirable, though his firmness flagged when Nell suddenly became aware of my haversack.

"You are not leaving us, Dulac?"

"Duty calls. It has even come to seek me out."

Then she turned to Peakes, and with a furious fluttering of eyelashes, asked him for news from the front.

The news was not good. The action had shifted southward, to the banks of the Somme, where the Germans, dug deep in their shelters some forty feet beneath the ground, had remained untouched by the four million shells we had rained down on them. Refusing to admit defeat, the British generals had ordered their troops to advance—in closed ranks, as if on parade, for decorum had to be respected whatever the cost. The enemy didn't even have to aim to mow them down. A half-hour later, nineteen thousand dead and thirty-eight thousand wounded lay entangled in the barbed wire of no-man's-land. Of the Newfoundland Regiment, only a handful remained.

Now the British had withdrawn, and were waiting for the Canadians to relieve them. We feared the worst. Carpenters were already at work, cobbling together crude coffins. And the medical services had been issued orders to outfit three new casualty clearing stations manned by specialized teams of surgeons, anesthesists and nurses.

Nell, who had been listening to his devastating account with near-enthusiastic interest, suddenly interrupted the lieutenant.

"I too am leaving for the Somme tomorrow. I've had enough of tucking in sheets and plumping pillows. I have requested my transfer to a field ambulance, and my request has been accepted."

Apparently, to be one of the twelve chosen to serve close to the front lines was the ambition of every nurse, equivalent to the highest military honour.

"If they are anticipating as many wounded as you claim, lieutenant, the physicians will be overwhelmed, and they will certainly allow me to suture wounds. Your thimble will come in handy."

The moment of parting had come, and Peakes turned to me with a sinister smile.

"Make your farewells to Miss Nell."

I stepped toward her and held out my hand.

"Until we meet again, then?"

They say that revenge is a dish best eaten cold. How long had Peakes been staring at his plate before deciding to consume it? Impossible to know, but he certainly bit into it ferociously. Stepping confidently between Nell and me, he slapped me hard on the back.

"I hope you haven't become too attached to your patient, Nell. Don't forget that his wife and children are waiting for him back in Manitoba."

I felt the ground open beneath my feet, and a wave of vertigo sweep over me. Every lie is like a thick fog, and the man who would make his way through that fog must be prepared to run headlong into the wall of truth at any time. Yet I was not prepared, and it took me several moments to realize what had hit me, during which time I came close to hating Peakes. But the admiration I couldn't help feeling for his detective's flair and tenacity quickly took the upper hand.

What could have possibly set him on that trail? Not I, certainly. I had not indicated I was married on my recruitment application. On the orders of the Minister of War, all heads of families were obliged to obtain the consent of their wives before joining—and I had preferred to confront mine with a *fait accompli*. My very irregular correspondence with her had always been reserved, hardly propitious for displays of emotion. Even if the lieutenant had got his hands on a few letters, he would have been hard pressed to read anything more between the lines than the obligatory, conventional exchange between brother and sister, whom time has long separated. To learn the truth, he would have had to deploy an entire arsenal of resources, and carry his investigation back to High Bluff.

He had indeed put me in a difficult situation with his rather theatrical revelation. But could Nell be angry at me for not tipping my hand?

The answer to that question was in her eyes. They were rippling with fury, like the face of a hostile sea. With a brisk salute to Peakes, she withdrew on the pretext that she had to treat her hair against nits.

"You know, if one sleep with dogs, one must expect to wake up with fleas."

I picked up my haversack and prepared to follow the lieutenant. But he was intent on rubbing it in.

"Your ring finger betrayed you, Dulac. It's thinner where you used to wear your wedding band."

How could I have forgotten? Gold always leaves a trail.

XXV

WHAT IS THE PROBABILITY of two shells bursting in exactly the same place? It was a question I often asked myself as I surveyed the crater-riddled battlefields. I can now answer with certainty: it is the same as the probability of lightning striking the same man twice.

For several weeks now, Peakes and I had been combing the backroads of the Somme in a tiny patrol vehicle, complete with capricious motor and slipping clutch. The villages we passed through resembled one another as much in their desolate appearance as in the monotony of their names: Eaucourt, Beaucourt, Commécourt, Gomiécourt, Frémicourt, Fricourt, Bihucourt, Beaulencourt, Warlencourt, Bancourt, Rancourt, Bouzincourt, Haplincourt, Riencourt, Gueudecourt ... In such circumstances, time seems to stand still.

Yet Peakes had rarely been in such fine fettle. He who laughs last, laughs best. Once he had kept me under close watch out of superstition; today, it was out of pure malevolence. His pride spoke of settled accounts. For him, the great day of retribution had come. To have discredited me in front of Nell was not enough. No. He was determined that I feel the full weight of my defeat with the well aimed, heavy-handed blows of his sarcasm. I could have done without his remarks on the advantages of celibacy, and his questions dripping with false solicitude. What was the latest news from

Mrs. Dulac, and how were the children? Wasn't I anxious to see my family again? I was indulgent; I let him talk. Why would he hold his tongue? It was all part of the game. All things considered, his intervention had proved opportune. My mind, freed from the passion that had too long distracted it from its true aims, could now be mustered to help me accomplish my quest.

During our interminable patrols, I had ample occasion to reflect upon the connections that might exist between the paving stone at Rouge-Croix, the Templar sites of Flanders and the holy places of Jerusalem. I came to understand how Godefroy de St. Omer, who held a secret of inestimable worth, had conceived a hiding place as secure as the crypts that lay beneath the ancient Temple of Solomon, which had resisted for centuries.

Such a great treasure warranted nothing less. The knight had resolved to transform all Flanders into a kind of new Jerusalem. He had first established eight Templar commanderies, whose respective locations had been chosen to replicate the map of the eight Christian sites of the Holy City. Thus the commandery of Ypres stood for the Patriarchate, that of Aire-sur-la-Lys for Sainte Marie of the Latins, that of Lomme for the Holy Sepulchre and so on.

This was just the map that Godefroy had had engraved on the floor of the cistern of the largest commandery of Flanders, that of Cæstre, in the locality of Rouge-Croix. But to safeguard the secret, the additional circle that indicated the town of Saint Omer, which stood for the palace of King Baudoin, had been indicated by a simple, crowned B. Once aware of this tenuous connection, an initiate could establish a direct correspondence between the Duchy of Flanders and Jerusalem, and thus deduce, by following the trail of clues, the location of the treasure. At least, that was how I, Simon Dulac, a non-initiate, had discovered Godefroy's secret.

If I were not mistaken—and it would surprise me if I were—the treasure was to be found in the Flemish commandery that occupied, on the map, the same position as the site in which it had been discovered: the ancient Temple of Solomon, seat of the Templars in Jerusalem. The commandery that had been so designated belonged to Arras.

My quest had begun to resemble a game of hopscotch. Who could tell if, having reached my goal, a new clue would not send me off in an entirely different direction? Such were my thoughts as I bounced up and down on the seat of the patrol vehicle.

For the time being, I was a good twenty miles south of Arras, on the road to Auchonvillers, which the British pronounced *Ocean Villas*—just as they massacred the names of Ypres (*Wipers*), Cæstre (*Castor*), Armentières (*Arm Chair*), Fleurbaix (*Flower Beds*), Ficheux (*Fish Hooks*) and Norrent-Fontes (*No Refunds*). The trip was made longer by Peakes, who stopped every hundred feet, having imagined some deserter crouched in the thickets. I beat the bushes with him—why protest as long as the action moved northward?

Dusk had not yet fallen, but the artillery had begun its nightly barrage when our vehicle bogged down. I told Peakes to stay put, I would get out and push. The problem was minor. One of the wheels had slipped over the edge of a shell hole, and I quickly freed it. The vehicle lurched forward with a cough. Instead of running to catch up, I motioned Peakes to wait. I thought I had seen something gleaming at the bottom of the hole.

It was a meadowlark's nest, made of twigs, moss and dried peat, woven together with strands of barbed wire. Peakes, who had ambled over, let out a chuckle of satisfaction when he saw it.

"I told you so, Dulac! The new Iron Age is upon us! Not even the birds can escape it."

As if nature were confirming his words, a melodious warbling rose up. But the sound was continuous, and coming closer. Suddenly I realized, rather too late, that it was not the song of the meadowlark.

I ran for the automobile. The lieutenant wanted to save the nest, and climbed down into the hole instead of following me.

The shell struck the road with such force that I was thrown over the hood of the vehicle. As for the lieutenant, he had managed to flee the point of impact, and was still alive when I found him. But in what a state! Where his mustache had been, there was a metal plate so red that the flesh smoked around it. His jaw hung about his neck, and his throat gaped open like the beak of a fledgling awaiting its meal. As for the rest of his features, I could make out only the whites of his eyes, floating amid the fast-coagulating blood.

When he saw me, he began to gesticulate—he wanted to write something. I had neither pencil nor paper. With a trembling finger, he wrote these words in the mud: "*What perils do environ ...* " And I replied, aloud, "The man who meddles with cold iron."

XXVI

THE BUGLE HAD SOUNDED roll-call at two o'clock in the
morning. I had selected ten new recruits from among the men
of the company and handed them rifles. Then, with no
explanation, I brought them to an abandoned farm three miles
from Vimy. I ordered them to stand to attention at the far end
of the barnyard and wait in silence.

In the distance, a cock crowed. The vapour rising from the
earth spread and hung over the ground, a sign that another
foggy day was in store. A truck sped into the barnyard,
followed by an ambulance. I turned to the men of the
detachment and reminded them that it was Holy Saturday.

The drivers pulled a soldier from the truck. Blindfolded,
hands and feet in shackles, he wore a cardboard target pinned
to the left side of his chest. Beside him walked a chaplain,
chanting *De Profundis*. Behind me, the recruits began to fidget
when they realized that an execution was about to take place.

I stepped forward to read the sentence.

"The court martial has found the accused guilty of
cowardice in the face of the enemy, and has condemned him
to death by firing squad."

The prisoner stretched his neck left and right, like a blind-
man's bluff player trying to peek out from under his blindfold.
I recognized the bloke—a hefty chap who had spent his life
working in the salt mines before signing on as a sapper. I had

often encountered him in the houses of ill repute, where I never failed to catch him cheating. I had seen him another time, in the Bois du Sanctuaire, when the Germans had used flame-throwers for the first time. Every single man in the squad had been burned alive except him. So impregnated with salt was his skin that the flames had not even singed it. The only water I could offer him was at the bottom of a jerry can, and it stunk of gasoline. He drank it anyway, and then, with a rueful look, showed me his loaded dice misshapen by the heat.

I had arrested him myself in the field ambulance where he had gone for treatment. I was not about to forget the incident for, as the guards were taking him away, whom should I encounter but Nell? Hands thrust into a muff that matched her Astrakhan cap, her feet perched atop two bayonet blades, she was skating across a frozen puddle. She nearly toppled into my arms.

"What will they do to the man who's been arrested?"

Under the new regulations, even minor infringements, such as leaving one's post or returning a few hours late from leave, were now considered as attempted desertion, and punished with the same severity as the most serious crimes. It so happened that the prisoner had deliberately inoculated himself in the eye with syphilis in order to be sent home. The death sentence was automatic.

"He will probably be executed."

Nell had seemed as relieved as she did distressed. She had just lost a considerable sum to the sapper at dice, and he had threatened to cut off her little finger if she didn't pay up.

"Why even play with that individual? Everyone knows he's a swindler."

"If you're going to lose, you may as well lose big."

"You should learn to select your opponents more carefully."

"I don't want to play hard to get, Dulac. After all, I'm a kind of no-man's-land myself—what you might politely call a surplus woman. I take whatever I can get: swindlers, liars, unfaithful husbands ... "

As a reproach, it was spoken with a certain indulgence, rather like a fault half-forgiven. Which proves that distance is to a woman's anger what air is to a flame. Too little fans it, while too much can extinguish it.

"It was a simple oversight."

"An oversight is also a lie. And lying is against orders."

"Impose a pledge, and we shall be even."

"Exemplary punishment is called for, proportional to the crime. I can think of nothing less than dancing at the end of a rope. Unless you reveal to me a secret that you have never revealed to anyone else."

I took her by the arm and led her toward the automobile.

"Where are you taking me?"

"It doesn't matter, as long as it's intimate."

She asked me to wait. Her watch would soon begin, and she had to find an excuse for her absence. A few minutes later she reappeared, an insouciant will-o'-the-wisp in the bellicose night. She slipped across the front seat and came to rest against me.

"What lie did you tell them?"

"That the military police wanted to interrogate me about the prisoner."

All the while avoiding the troops streaming toward Vimy Ridge, we turned onto a road spiked with sharp stones. Nell, who enjoyed turbulence, let herself be rocked by the motion of the car. At the end of a private road, we came upon an abandoned villa. The entire façade had collapsed, but the interior was untouched. It looked like the cross-section of a doll's house, with the bedroom upstairs, the ground-floor living room, and all the miniature furniture, the armchairs, the over-mantle chimney and the stairway still intact.

Nell, it goes without saying, insisted we go upstairs. I feigned an attack of vertigo, for the room seemed to be suspended in mid-air, and skilfully I guided her bedward. As I went to unbutton my fly, she stopped me.

"That's not the kind of secret I had in mind."

I had only one secret—and it was not for the sharing. I tried to outwit her, to avoid the issue, but she was not prepared to bargain. If I insisted, she would only become more obstinate, and I, less satisfied.

Where had this iron will of hers come from? Nell's very appearance seemed to have hardened since St. Omer. Her skin had bronzed in the open air, her features had become sharper, her temples had turned silver. Even the tiny beauty spot on her chin had taken on the armour-like sheen of hematite. Her voice held new tones of irony as well. She seemed to have been tempered, as I now was learning at some expense.

The occasional gust of wind shook the walls and caused the remains of the chimney to crack. Nell complained of the cold, even as I was embracing her thighs the way you would grasp an armful of lilacs. To attain my ends, perhaps I could ill afford not to disclose the riddle, but nothing obliged me to reveal the solution.

"If I tell you my secret, will you give yourself to me?"

"I shall do better than that. I will show you my original stain."

"Done!"

Immediately, I gave her the sheet of paper on which I had reproduced the design on the paving stone, explaining that I had found these mysterious signs in the cellars at Rouge-

Croix. Nose in the air, she put on her little Miss Know-It-All face.

"Pretty enough, but there is nothing mysterious about it."

I must confess that I had a moment of doubt. What had I overlooked that Nell had so easily recognized?

She spread the drawing out on the bed, and as if to make it clear she was lowering herself to my level, she leaned over me, and in an exaggerated manner, began to play the teacher. The large upper and lower forms were cylinders, with their notched frets and pawls, each connected by pegs to the heddles. In the middle, one could clearly make out the leash rod that separated the warp from the weft. Wasn't it all perfectly clear? No, it wasn't. My silence made that much obvious. She sighed with exasperation; she would have to employ simpler terms if I was to understand her demonstration.

"The diagram illustrates the mechanism of a high-warp loom. As anyone can see, the threads of the warp are vertically, not horizontally disposed, which gives a tighter weave, and a more accurate design. Which is why high-warp looms are used for silk, gold and silver."

I may not have known much about weaving, but Nell had not a clue about treasure maps. Her hypothesis was quite preposterous, and I quickly explained why. The Templars were knights, not craftsmen. What connection could they possibly have with the craft of weaving?

She was not to be dissuaded.

"To my understanding, they were the ones who initiated the Flemish weavers into the secrets of the high-warp loom. How do you think the West discovered chain mail, buttons, the lute and the mattress? By rummaging through the great booty that the Crusaders brought back from the Holy Land."

"But why carve such a plan in stone?"

"In those days, a new weaving technique was as precious as a new weapon. The proof? Think of cities like Ypres and Arras, that became rich and powerful. And in any event, what else could it possibly be?"

I was certainly not about to say *a treasure map*.

"A rebus, perhaps?"

Not only had I silenced her, I had aroused her curiosity. She set herself to scrutinizing the diagram again, turning it this way and that way. At the apex of her eyebrows, the three tiny wrinkles that formed a palm leaf reappeared, for the solution was no more apparent to her than it was to me. Then suddenly, her face lit up, and I thought for a moment that she had found the answer. Not at all. It had simply occurred to her that if anyone could elucidate the mystery, it would be Lieutenant Peakes.

Peakes. The king of cryptograms, and living proof that the human body could survive the direst mutilations. I thought he had been transferred to London, to one of those hospitals where the surgeons were now able to reconstruct throats, devise artificial jaws, remodel torn cheeks with wax. From Nell I learned that he had chosen to remain in Arras while he waited for the prosthetic service to build him a silver-plated, sheet-metal mask, shaped and hand-painted to resemble an old photograph of himself.

"The resemblance to his real face is uncanny. With his mask, the lieutenant will always have the same features he had before the war. It will almost be as if it never happened."

I did not care for that protective tone of voice of hers; it made me suspect she had decided once and for all to take the lieutenant under her wing. Still, she had not forgotten her promise to show me her birthmark, and wished to do so, here and now. But judging from the way she refused to meet my gaze, I was almost certain that her true intention was to trick me.

I propped myself up on my elbow, curious to see how she would go about it. She opened her mouth wide and I saw, on her soft palate, a dark, almost black mark. It was not at all what I had hoped for, but I stared at it at length, fascinated by the workings of chance.

In the barnyard of the old farm, on the road to Vimy, the chaplain blessed the prisoner for a final time. The firing squad took aim, and I gave the order to fire. My voice was muffled by the crack of the rifles, one of which had fired a blank cartridge. On the ground where a few seconds ago a man had stood, there was nothing but a heap of flannel toward which the surgeon and the stretcher-bearers were now making their way. I checked my watch.

"The sentence was carried out at ten minutes after four this morning."

In the ranks, not a word was spoken on the return to barracks. The conscripts had received the message: once the great game of war began, there was nothing to be gained by cheating.

XXVII

BY THE DIM LIGHT of a lantern, I began the descent into obscurity. Nell followed close behind, negotiating her way cautiously down the steep and slippery slope of the narrow gallery that wound down into the rock.

The entire city of Arras lies atop a subterranean twin—hundreds of caverns hollowed out by quarrymen over the course of centuries from an immense limestone deposit. Because of their constant temperature, these alcoves, as they were called hereabouts, were most often used as storage cellars. At the beginning of the hostilities, the army had requisitioned the uppermost level for use as a main dressing station. It was there that the more than six thousand Canadian wounded in the first week of fighting at Vimy were evacuated. But the sub-cellar had not been put to use. We would not be disturbed.

For several days I had been exploring this underground labyrinth, but I had not yet been to this particular spot. The gallery opened out into a vault the ceiling of which was supported by sandstone pillars. It could very well have been a chapel, minus the odour of burning tapers. We must have been a good forty feet beneath the rue des Teinturiers—far enough distant from the wards that there was little risk of being discovered.

As I lifted the hem of Nell's coif to breathe in the perfume of her neck, she took the lantern from me and made her way forward among the pillars. As she walked, her rump swayed so gracefully that I could not take my eyes off her. I followed close behind, slipping along the face of the rough rock wall. Careless of where I was going, I collided with a bottle rack that shuddered, then began to sway and totter. Before I could catch it, it toppled onto the floor with a crash that echoed through the subterranean chambers.

I had just enough time to hug the wall to avoid being crushed by the rack, and as I did, my shoulder sunk into something thick and velvety in texture. Suddenly, the flame of the lantern flickered in the darkness, but not because of a draft. It was my little bluebird's hand trembling.

"I always knew that with your luck, you'd end up unearthing a tapestry for me."

Against the rock wall, in the crevice that had been hidden by the bottle rack, a massive wall hanging was suspended, almost as tall as the ceiling. Though its hues of crimson and emerald green had lost their ancient splendour, the details had conserved all their accuracy. Against a background of flowering greenery, it depicted an abundance of richly feathered birds, with their sharp beaks, their gleaming eyes, their lacquered claws, their ruffed crests. Here was a pheasant; there, a trumpeter swan. Two sandpipers on legs like stalks of bamboo; flocks of sparrows; a peacock about to spread his tail; an owl; a goose extending its wings protectively over an albino blackbird; several parakeets, their flamboyant heads protruding from a nest on which was perched a woodpecker; the obligatory eagle and pigeon as well.

An expression of gravitas came over Nell's features, one that surprised me. She pressed her body against mine. The tapestry, she said, bore the signature of the master weavers of Arras, whose fame was so great in England and Italy that their hangings were known simply by the names *arras* and *arazzi*. But I could not make out a signature anywhere.

"You can recognize them by the lacy outline of the lily-of-the-valley leaves."

The flowers on the tapestry were not lily-of-the valley, but polygonatums, I corrected her. The woods near High Bluff were full of them, and I had frequently unearthed their long white rhizomes in the course of my digging.

"Lily-of-the-valley or polygonatums, what difference does it make?"

"On their roots, where the shoots have fallen off, there are round scar markings like seals. That's why they're commonly called Solomon's Seal ... This allusion to the builder of the Temple is no coincidence. If you want my opinion, the Templars have already come this way."

"What if the entire tapestry were a rebus?"

Gently I lifted her chin, and brushed her tiny beauty spot.

"Nell, you see rebuses everywhere."

"Don't blame me. In Arras, they *are* everywhere."

What I did not know is that the rebus was born here—an invention of the medieval clerics, who had devised a concise method of circulating their satirical epigrams during Carnival.

"The practice quickly spread throughout the city," Nell told me. "The result? All the sculpted insignia that you see above the gates of the Grand'Place are rebuses. Once they identified the merchants whose commerces were located there. There were golden lions, falling stars, checkerboards, each representing the trade practiced within, from the inn where one sleeps well to the house of ill-repute. Everyone believes that *La Dame à la licorne, Les Instruments de la Passion,*

L'Offrande du cœur, Les Neuf Preux, Le Bal des Sauvages or *La Baillée des roses* are allegories. But I can prove that the images conceal a hidden message."

I needed no more urging than that to unroll the tapestry. I clambered onto the fallen bottle-rack, but as I reached toward the top of the wall, Nell clutched my leg.

"Don't touch it."

"We found it. It belongs to us. Whatever falls into the trench is fair game for the soldier."

"It has no gold threads, Dulac."

"Do you think I want to burn it?"

"Accidents happen in the twinkling of an eye."

"At least let me unroll it for you, so you can examine it more closely."

The hanging, which must have been accumulating dust for centuries, was as heavy as a carpet, and I needed all the help Nell could provide to lift it. Once stretched out on the floor, it no longer seemed as imposing as when it had hung from the wall. It amounted to little more than the spread of a nuptial bed—not counting the fact that we had involuntarily placed it wrong side up.

"Wait."

Nell did not want me to turn it over immediately. Kneeling at the foot of the tapestry, she moved the lamp from bird to bird, as though reading from a large open book.

"I see, I see."

"Is there a secret message?"

She did not answer. For what she saw, and what transfigured her, was the reverse of the tapestry—that second face that, contrary to the disappointing canvas backing of embroidery, is quite as sumptuous as the first, from which it differed in no way whatsoever, were it not for the tiny, visible knots in which the threads of various colours established their secret ties. The penumbra of the vault brought out its relief as it accentuated the texture of Nell's skin. Flesh and plumage became so blurred that my eye all but lost sight of my beautiful bluebird among the other occupants of that vivid aviary. Yet it was her fine fabric, with all its softness and yielding, that my hand encountered each time it slipped beneath her bodice.

But I could advance no farther. Nell's entire body stiffened, and her face seemed to withdraw behind a curtain of iron that bore the tarnish of reproach—of rancour too, perhaps. I should not have disturbed her in her contemplation. I discreetly withdrew, but she held me back with a smile.

"And now, for a rebus."

I held the lamp high as she set about enumerating the birds. She recited their names in the chirping voice that they themselves might use, gently modulating the sound as she toyed with their order.

"A turnstone, a gannet, a heron, a crossbill, a goldeneye ... "

Like a flight of birds, her words took to the air, soaring up to the ceiling of the vault, fluttering there for a moment, then suddenly changing direction. When they swooped back upon me in fresh order, I thought I could make out new echoes in their song.

"A heron, a turnstone, a crossbill, a gannet, a goldeneye"

I could not understand everything, but the real meaning could not escape me. I picked up the words "stone to be turned," "cross" and, above all, "gold."

My heart was beating furiously, and it was all I could do to restrain myself as Nell recited the secret message in its entirety.

Here, on turning stone, cross and bill cannot gold deny.

I allowed myself to interrupt her. "Are you sure you're not mistaken?"

She gave me a black look, as if to doubt her the minutia of her work was an insult. Yet she was the one who was perplexed. Because though she could easily read the rebus, she manifestly could not understand its meaning. For me, everything was clear. The encrypted message that Godefroy had had woven into the tapestry provided all the clues we needed to locate the treasure.

Our first step was to find the turning stone. Where else could it be than in the Abbey of Saint Vaast, on the rue des Teinturiers, located directly above our heads? There we would find a carved cross and bill. I supposed that by causing the stone to turn in the same direction as the sign of the cross, a mechanism would be activated, and that beneath the rotating stone would lie a hoard of gold for the taking.

Once again, fortune's grace had descended upon me. There was no doubt in my mind: I was indeed one of its chosen few. Lady Luck would not abandon me now, as I was about to fulfill my destiny. I could hear the gold summoning me from above, I could feel the warm rays of its munificence, my eyes were dazzled by its glitter. So strong was my exultation that it overflowed my body. Though it was hardly the moment, I could not stop paying Nell the most impudent compliments, and outlining the unmentionable excesses we could commit in celebration of this red-letter day. In reply, she pointed out that it was becoming increasingly difficult to see in the underground vault.

It was true enough. The lamp had burned low. Were it to flicker out, it would become extremely difficult to find our way back through the labyrinth of alcoves—with or without dice. I hurriedly rolled up the tapestry and stowed it in a corner. Nell suddenly became agitated.

"You're not going to hang it up again?"

"Be reasonable. We have just enough time to return to the entrance."

"It'll bring us bad luck."

"Don't worry. I assume full responsibility."

"Don't say I didn't warn you."

We made our way through the gallery by which we had come. Nell was far from reassured. She bit her lips, glanced back over her shoulder, then quickened her pace. Her disquiet was beginning to affect me, too. The incline was steep, and I was short of breath. Why does the road back always seem so much longer?

Finally we reached the surface. Night had fallen, and my breath came easier. At the far end of the rue des Teinturiers, the ruins of the Abbey of Saint Vaast, destroyed by the war, stood in silhouette, black against a dark sky. Unimaginable luck would be needed if we were to find a tiny inscription in that heap of rubble. But the treasure was there, I could feel it. Its defenses had been shaken by the bombardment, its last resistance was weakening; at the first encounter with a more powerful will, it would be forced to reveal itself. If I could trust my intuition, it contained prodigious riches.

My little bluebird, insensible to the vibrations of gold, had already turned toward the Grand'Place, without so much as a glance at the Abbey. She did not have to tell me where she was going. I knew that, every evening, she went to visit Peakes, who was recovering from his wounds in a house with a gabled façade.

I would rather she say nothing to him, but that, I realized, was impossible. She was still intrigued by the first part of the rebus, and unlike me, who had no objection at all to leaving it a mystery, she needed to solve it immediately. In what form would we find the gold? That was what she wanted to know.

"Perhaps it is a cloth of gold?"

That's Nell for you. Show her a treasure, and all she'll care about is a length of embroidered rag. As if Godefroy de St. Omer had set out in pursuit of frills and flounces.

"And if it were really the Veil of the Temple?"

According to Nell, the Veil of the Temple was a great purple curtain upon which King Solomon had caused a thousand cherubim to be woven in purest gold thread—a tapestry, in other words. Rent asunder from top to bottom by a mysterious force at the very instant Christ expired, the veil had disappeared forever when the legions of Emperor Titus burned Jerusalem and massacred all its inhabitants, twenty-six years later.

Nell, of course, was convinced that the veil had not been destroyed along with the city, but had been removed for safe keeping to the imperial stables where, one thousand years later, the Templars would discover it and transport it to Flanders. She was prepared to wager that by studying it closely, Flemish weavers discovered the art of tapestry and developed the high-warp loom. Through the veil of her obsession, Nell could see only cloth.

It seemed unlikely to me that the treasure of the Templars was actually a tapestry, but I was prepared to accept all possibilities. In the Temple, the veil had shrouded the Holy of Holies—a perfect cube measuring thirty feet on all sides— from the eyes of the profane. Which meant the veil itself would have to be thirty feet long and thirty feet wide.

Nine hundred square feet of gold thread ... How much would that be, in ingots? By burning the tapestry, I should be able to recover a small fortune.

XXVIII

BY THE LIGHT OF EARLY MORNING, the ruins of the Abbey seemed to have thrust up, jagged and gloomy, in a single upheaval. The filaments of cirrus clouds that passed overhead were caught in their crown of thorns and torn. I made my way into the cloister through the side door of the cathedral after having clambered over the collapsed, vaulted roof of the peristyle. I am speaking, of course, of the great, not the small, cloister. For the Abbey of Saint Vaast had been entirely rebuilt in the eighteenth century by Cardinal de Rohan—the notoriously libertine clergyman who had been involved in the Collier affair with the Conte di Cagliostro. Had his Italian accomplice, an infamous Freemason, passed on to the Cardinal certain secrets relating to the Abbey, or had the monks themselves warned him against touching the great cloister? Whatever the case may be, during the course of the work the Cardinal insisted that the inner courtyard be left untouched, and above all, that the modest cross of iron planted in its centre be preserved. This much the sacristan of the cathedral had revealed to me. Such scruples, unusual for a prince of the Church with regard to an object of so little value, were in themselves sufficient to awaken my treasure-hunter's sixth sense.

The cross, just as the sacristan had told me, was hardly worth a glance. It was made of wrought iron, and badly rusted.

Still, not even the bombardment had toppled it from its stone pedestal, an ancient millstone upon which could be made out, in Carolingian script, the words *Sursum corda*. Uplift our hearts ...

At first glance, there was no bill, nor turning stone on the pedestal beneath the cross. Nor was there at second glance. Push and shake the cross, kick the pedestal though I might, I could induce no movement, nor hear any sound of stone turning upon stone. What I did hear was a cackle as abrasive as a leper's rattle.

I was not alone. Someone had passed through the fallen arches and was making his way across the inner courtyard. I recognized him: the spectre of defeat. His rapier-like silhouette moved toward me with a duelist's sprightly step. The rising sun, about to peep over the ruins, would soon strike him full in the face.

In two years of war, I had seen the thousand faces of the wounded. The purulent cutaneous excrescences left by mustard gas, the sharp-edged cavities sliced through the skin by rifle and machine-gun bullets, the huge, fist-shaped pouches gouged out by shrapnel. The grenade wounds encrusted with dirt and shredded cloth, the deep furrows ploughed by the bayonet exposing the glass-like surface of bone and the knobs of cartilage. The mincemeat of the internal organs ... But I had yet to witness the appearance of those wounds once healed, when the abominable scar tissue, unpolished in texture and silvery in its reflections, finally took the place of vanished flesh.

So this is what had become of Peakes's lacerated face. I wondered if the lieutenant had had the courage to look at himself in a mirror of late. And, supposing that he had, how those distortions now weighed upon his soul, now that he knew that he looked for all the world like a gargoyle.

Of all possible mutilations, that which he had suffered must be the worst cross to bear. For what could be the loss of an arm or leg, compared to the disfiguration of that part of one's self offered to the eyes of the world?

I marveled, above all, at the physical prodigy that allowed his jawless head to stay atop his peg-like neck. At any moment, I could swear, it looked as though it would roll off onto his shoulder, there to dangle from the slender thread of an artery.

As if to keep me from penetrating the mystery, Peakes ran his hand over his face, and with the quickness of a shell-game artist, made it reappear whole, as human as if the shrapnel had never ripped it away.

Nell had told me that Peakes had taken to wearing an iron mask. But the one he had slipped on had none of the rigidity of a metallic prosthesis. It hung like a well-cut tail-coat, or a rich tapestry, and when its heavy folds undulated in the wind, the outline of his lips formed first a smile, then an evil grin, both giving his pallid skin the finely-calibrated, ever-changing degrees of sanguinity that reflected emotion. No need to wonder who the author of the mask was, not when I saw that it was made of minuscule points, embroidered and re-embroidered with the finest silken thread.

"Nell really fixed your face for you, lieutenant! You were never that handsome before."

By way of reply, he handed me the slate that hung from his neck.

Find anything interesting?

"This hasn't been my lucky day, if that makes you feel better."

He raised his eyebrows, the sole means of expression that remained, then rubbed his slate clean with the whitened sleeve of his military tunic, and scribbled a few words with a stub of chalk.

No coded message in tapestry. Nell made it all up.

I would have liked to deny it, and prove him wrong, but the evidence for his assertion lay before my eyes, in the rusty iron cross in the courtyard, and I could no longer pretend to be surprised. Yes, she had made a fool of me, that unmitigated little barnyard strumpet, with her tapestries and her rebuses, her herons and her turnstones, her crossbills and her goldeneyes, that might just as well have been boobies, fly-catchers, anhingas and a gaggle of cackling geese for all that it mattered.

I sat down among the columns, on the low rock wall, unconcerned that Peakes was witnessing my discouragement. What had become of my pride?

"I can't believe that I'll have fought this damnable war without anything to show for it."

The slate fell at my feet.

Nell is nothing?

I picked it up, rubbed it clean with my kerchief and handed it back to Peakes.

"Nell is a no-man's-land—a danger zone where the heart beats faster, a place for furtive incursions only."

The lieutenant sat down beside me. Bent over, chalk stub in hand, he wrote and wrote. What was he doing? Telling his life story?

I've discovered the solution to the riddle of Rouge-Croix. I give it to you in exchange for Nell.

It was hard to trust someone who had tried to shoot me in the back. But it just might be my last chance ...

Iacta alea est. Fortune, let me be your fool! The costly pact I concluded with Peakes seemed, for the moment, to be no more than a source of regret. Would I never see Nell again? Never write to her? Must I forget her very name? No doubt I would eventually have my recompense. Ten months later. On November 1. That was our agreement.

For me, the lure of the quest would always be more powerful than the thrill of conquest.

XXIX

One afternoon, I was drinking with a group of officers in a public house in Lillers when one of my men came knocking at the door. He insisted on speaking to me. With no small irritation, I stepped outside. A local cock breeder had organized a fight for us, and I'd bet heavily on a rusty-gold bird that had been duly stuffed with garlic to drive it to a frenzy. The creature had already managed to deliver its opponent several brutal blows with its iron gaffs, but the other cock had a sharpened beak, and my bird was bleeding from his barbs.

Keeping an eye on the events in the pit, I asked the sergeant what he wanted. He proudly announced that he had arrested a lady spy. I was not excessively alarmed. Ever since the execution of Mata Hari, my men were seeing female spies everywhere. As the reward for a successful capture was two weeks' leave in London, they were quite prepared to arrest whatever chickadee so much as showed a bit of leg.

"Where is she?"

"Just outside, lieutenant. Under guard."

When he addressed me as "lieutenant," I thought immediately of Peakes. I still hadn't become accustomed to being addressed that way.

Through the window I could see a crowd of curious passers-by milling about in the square: housewives in their aprons, apprentices perched on the top step of their shops, more than a few troopers with their mules. All of them were gaping at the prisoner who stood there, hands bound, between two hefty guards. Several of the onlookers were laughing maliciously, and others had begun to hiss. The women were particularly vindictive, insulting her by calling out the names of birds. Where had they learned such vulgar language?

But the spittle of those toads appeared not to touch the white dove, who rose above the mêlée by raising her eyes skyward, far beyond the rooftops. It was the same confident gaze, the same hope-filled attitude that she had displayed at Trincques—the only other occasion on which I had met her after my pact with Peakes.

Let us say, more properly, on which I had caught sight of her. It was Dominion Day, and to celebrate the founding of our nation, the fifty thousand men of the three Canadian divisions had been invited to witness an exhibition of aerial acrobatics. As the throb of the approaching engines grew louder, they all raised their heads at once, and as the biplanes turned loop-the-loops and barrel rolls, I suddenly saw the white wings of a nursing sister's coif among the undifferentiated khaki of thousands of forage caps.

I had no sooner recognized Nell's aquiline profile than she turned in my direction. Even in the crowd, she had spotted me easily, perhaps because she had been looking for me. Any moment now, she would make her way to the spot where I stood, and speak to me, and I, instead of returning her pleasantries, would be forced to inform her that the game was over.

To the best of my recollection, I have never fled in the face of the enemy, but when Nell took a few steps in my direction, I stepped back an equal distance. Not only did I fear meeting her face to face, I felt that Peakes was spying on us, hidden behind his tapestry, and the words he had spoken at Messines came back to me. As he had predicted, the roles had been reversed. He now held the solution to the riddle and the high ground, and I who feared that the treasure would slip through my fingers could no longer take the game lightly. As beads of sweat bloomed on my forehead, I understood for the first time what it must have been like for those poor bastards I had threatened with death if they would not go over the top.

I believed I would never see Nell again, and I did not want to have as a last memory the faded image of the three tiny wrinkles in the shape of a palm leaf that had begun to darken her brow. Before her expression turned to one of recrimination, I turned on my heel and left.

Five months and twenty-four days had elapsed since my pact with Peakes. In exactly one week, the lieutenant would deliver his secret to me. Nell's reappearance, just as I was about to reach my goal, was hardly a positive sign.

Flanked by her two guards, she bore her ordeal patiently. She expected, no doubt, that I would quickly clear up the misunderstanding. From behind the window of the public house, I made no move at all, too disconcerted to realize how much I missed her liveliness, her playfulness, her spark. I was so preoccupied with finding a way to get rid of all these importune individuals in order to be alone with her that I almost forgot the sergeant who stood waiting, at attention, beside me.

"Where did you find her?"

"In a church. She was looking for tapestries, so she claims, except that she was absent without leave from her post, at the main dressing station."

"Why did you bring her here? You know the rules, don't you?"

"She claims she knows you, lieutenant. You can explain everything, she says."

Nell was beautiful, with her white forehead and pale gold locks bathing in the light of the autumn sun. I thought she could give her smile such sweetness only once, but there it was anew, repeated again and again. I felt more admiration than desire for her, so powerfully that I desired her as well, but in a different way.

"I do not know her."

"Are you certain?"

"If I had met her, I would have remembered. What evidence of espionage do you have against her?"

He handed me a folded piece of paper on which were drawn nine wheels with spokes.

"You can see how this aroused my suspicions, lieutenant. It seems to show the positions of our artillery. Do you think she was going to sell it to the enemy?"

"Better take no risks. Escort her to intelligence headquarters. They will interrogate her thoroughly."

I lingered a moment at the window as the sergeant marched back to his prisoner. I could not hear what he said, but it did not appear to please her. Before following him, she turned toward the public house, and her hawk's eye attempted to pierce the shadow in which I took refuge. She brandished her two manacled fists in my direction and, in a curse, raised the ring finger of her left hand. I could not see perfectly, but for a moment I would have sworn that she'd embroidered a gold ring on it.

When I returned back to my boon companions, the cockfight had just ended. The pit was littered with feathers and stained with blood. Bent over the body of his adversary, my cock crowed out his victory in a clarion voice.

XXX

ON THE MORROW we depart from Flanders, where I hope never to set foot again. Passchendaele has broken my hopes, and shattered my morale. My condition, worsened by the previous day's festive visit of Prince Amoradhat of Siam, has deteriorated even more sharply since the unexpected arrival of the Americans, those eleventh-hour heroes who absolutely insist on smiling at the top of their voices.

Our offensive was a disaster from beginning to end. The British commanding officers sent us into an ocean of mud that had already absorbed ninety million shells, and such quantities of mustard gas that the water lying stagnant in the craters was as corrosive as vitriol. In that soul-destroying blackness, thirty-five thousand men disappeared without a trace. Sucked down into the slime. A member of the general staff who had come to find out why the assault wave was not advancing, cried out, "For the love of God, have we truly sent our brave men into that swamp?" I had to inform him that it was worse further on.

Passchendaele: the Valley of the Passion. Assignment there was to be Nell's punishment for being absent without leave from her position for several hours. Perhaps an accusation of espionage and a court martial would have been better for her, though at the casualty clearing station to which she had been assigned—the one closest to the front lines—some overworked surgeon would probably have allowed her to use the technique of tapestry weaving to suture a few wounds.

She disappeared the day after the All Hallows' Eve truce, when the clearing station was obliterated in an air raid. The German Gothas had hit the tin roof marked with a red cross with such accuracy that the bombing had to have been deliberate. Several witnesses confirmed to those assigned to draw up casualty lists that they had seen the field hospital sink beneath the mud like a torpedoed vessel.

As it was going under, would Nell have tried to grasp whatever came to hand as a life-buoy? Before being carried away by the powerful, sucking current, would she have wondered if there was still hope for rescue? Some nights, I have a demented dream in which my little bluebird spreads her wings and takes flight. But immediately afterward, I see her buried up to her chest, struggling before being pulled inexorably downward, until all that remains on the surface of the mud is her head, then her face, then her white coif, then nothing.

That Peakes had taken pen and paper to convey the sad news astonished me at first. Then I understood his attempt to fill the abyss of his pain by speaking of Nell to someone who had known her as well as he had. He was wrong in that regard, for I knew nothing about her. Where did she come from? When had she begun to cast the dice? When had she learned to embroider? It never occurred to me to ask—yet it was not for lack of opportunity. I am not trying to lessen the burden on my conscience by blaming myself in ways that would be as futile as they are belated. I realize that I always preferred not to lift Nell's veil, at the risk of overlooking a treasure comparable to that of the Templars. In the end, Peakes caught her on the rebound, for no sooner had I turned my back than he and Nell announced their engagement. It would have been hard to believe had I not seen that finger which she insolently raised in my direction. Peakes? Why Peakes? Of all the fantasies my little bluebird might have had, that one has remained the most inexplicable.

On the last page of his letter, the lieutenant acknowledged that I had respected the conditions of our agreement, and as a man of honour, he fully intended to discharge his debt by delivering me the solution to the notorious riddle of the paving stone.

At first, I could not understand what he was getting at. He began by recounting that in Jerusalem, in the northwest corner of the site of the ancient Temple of Solomon, there once stood the terrifying Roman construction known as Antonia's Tower. Apparently, its vestiges are still visible beneath the present-day convent of the Sisters of Zion, and mark the first station for pilgrims making their way up the Via Dolorosa toward the Holy Sepulchre. From the convent, a stairway leads to a vaulted hall supported by pillars, where all that remains of the fortress is an archway of brick and a blank wall, as well as weep-holes through which rainwater is channeled into an underground cistern. On the floor lies an immense stone plaque called the Lithostrotos—the very place where Pilate condemned Christ, asking, "What is truth?" But that is not the only interesting aspect of this stone plaque. In certain places it bears curious markings, crudely chiseled into the rock. These markings form an arrangement of nine circles, some of which contain spoke-like motifs or crosses. One of them surrounds a crowned *B*, an arrangement identical to the one I found on the paving stone in Cæstre.

I did not stop to wonder what all this might signify. Hurriedly I read, consumed by impatience to find out what lay at the end, already prepared to resume my quest where Nell's little mystification had interrupted it. But I was quickly forced to slow down, such incredulity did the lines that followed arouse in me.

As Peakes would have it, when the ruins of Antonia's Tower were exhumed, a mere sixty years before, several dice made of bone, ivory and even glass were found strewn on the floor. Thanks to them, it was concluded that the markings represented the squares of a board game popular among members of the Roman garrison, the object of which was to reach the square containing a crowned "B." Not *B* as in Baphomet or Baudoin, but as in *Basileus*. The royal cast. The most sovereign cast of all. Most probably, it was at this king's game that the Roman soldiers had thrown lots for Christ's purple cloak after He had been stripped of his garments.

I still do not understand why it has taken me so long to accept this explanation. Such was the irony of the situation that even Peakes, in all his malevolence, could not possibly have devised a more thorough way of humiliating me.

So that was it. The great riddle of the Templars was nothing more than a dice game to divert a handful of legionaries stationed in Flanders, guarding against the Germanic invaders. Peakes had duly informed me that Cæstre had originally been a Roman fortress. Had I listened to him?

I had fancied myself the fair-haired child of fortune. As it turned out, I was fortune's fool. In a series of coincidences, I had seen the definitive proof of a hypothesis that was fundamentally erroneous, misshapen by my haste to find what I was seeking. When I came upon the round markings on the paving stone, I assumed they were the work of the Templars.

Certainly, the name of Rouge-Croix had led me astray. I did not yet know that everything that bears the red cross is not necessarily what it seems.

Here I was, back to square one, without the slightest idea of where to begin anew. Why not let chance decide? After all, my luck has not entirely deserted me. I was still a winner at dice. Tomorrow, we leave for Amiens, where there stands a cathedral whose treasure has long been lost ...

One day, I reflected, long after the war has ended, a gold-seeker will travel to Flanders and, drawn by vibrations from deep in the earth, will pause at Passchendaele. With the aid of his pick and shovel, he will exhume the remains of a nurse with a ring of gold thread on her finger. Neither Peakes nor I will be there to identify her. She will be buried alongside the other unknown soldiers, and on a small white cross will be written these words: *Known but to God.*